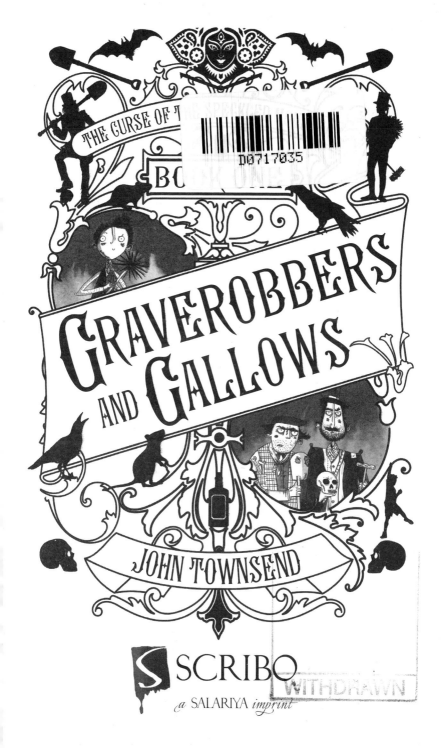

For the first ten years of my life I had nothing. Nothing at all in the world. And when you've got nothing in the world, you've got nothing in the world to lose. Apart from your life, of course... and I was ready to take the risk rather than do nothing. I was ready to risk anything. I was ready to risk losing life itself.

But then, surprisingly, something special came into my possession. I also acquired something that no one could ever take away. I learned to read. A new world opened up to me... and I uncovered a secret beyond my dreams. For the first time I glimpsed light, colour and truth in a dark, dismal, diseased age.

There was a time when it was dangerous to be a child. There was a time when no one dared tell their story. Now is the time to tell mine.

Cephas Catchpole

Cephas Catchpole

Cephas Catchpole, along with hundreds of other orphaned children, was just like Robert Blincoe (born around 1792 and thought to be the inspiration for Dickens's *Oliver Twist*).

By 1796 (that special year for medicine), Robert was living in a workhouse, with the fate of his parents unknown. At the age of only six, he was sent to work as a chimney boy, an assistant of a chimney sweeper, and his grim future seemed sealed. Cephas's story begins in very similar circumstances. Hope was all they had to cling to… it didn't let them down.

'No man dared to count his children as his own until they had had the disease (smallpox).'

Comte de la Condamine
(18th century mathematician and scientist)

'The havoc of the Plague visited our shores only once or twice within living memory; but the smallpox was always present, filling the churchyards with corpses.'

Thomas Macaulay, History of England, 1848

Early 1800s

─── *Chapter 1* ───

eing dead came as a terrible surprise. At first I assumed the room was blacker and colder than ever – until I opened my eyes and stirred... finding myself trapped inside a coffin. It didn't dawn on me that was my fate – lying, stunned as I was, in such solid darkness. The shock alone was enough to kill me when the penny finally dropped. Not that I had a penny to drop, never having owned a thing, let alone a coffin. And now, to crown it all,

it seemed I was declared dead, buried and pitifully extinct.

I had never imagined what it was like to be laid to rest in a grave. Not that there was time to dwell on such things, as I now had to face the stark truth that I would, indeed, be very dead very soon if I didn't get out very fast. My prospects did not look good – but they never had, at just ten years old and a penniless orphan, now with the added misfortune of being buried as a corpse. That was when it finally dawned on me that things could never get any worse. Little did I know they were about to.

At first I thought I was lying on a wooden floor at the dead of night, for I could only be sure of four things: my bed was very hard, I was freezing cold, I couldn't see a thing and I had a thumping headache. And that, for many minutes or maybe hours, was all I knew – as I drifted in and out of weird dreams.

Two distinct smells dragged me from sleep. One I knew only too well: soot. It was ingrained in my face, hair and often my throat – as with most of us chimney-sweep boys. The other smell was far sweeter; a flower. It wasn't from an expensive wreath of lilies but from some well-meaning soul who must have pushed a rose between my hands placed across my chest. For that was now all I could feel – thorns digging into my thumbs. That was what roused me to become fully awake and aware of the awful truth. That's when I lifted my head, cracked it on wood… and screamed like never before.

My shriek bounced back and filled the box in which I lay. That's when I knew I was buried in the earth, for the sound crashed back with such intensity – it had nowhere to escape. Beyond the wood was silent, solid oblivion. My entire world was solid – solid black and solid silence. The stale air seemed solid, too – closing in, like a slab pushing down on my face. So my own hands pushed upwards… pressing on the flimsy lid and clawing at the cheap timber, but it was useless. It just made me breathless and jabbed splinters under my sooty fingernails. I was completely helpless and my predicament hopeless. I was sure I'd never see daylight nor feel the sun on my face again. There was nothing I could do apart from weep. My short life was over and of all the ways it could end, why ever did it have to be like this?

The misty moon smeared its smoky light over the moss-clad church roof. Beyond the tower no glimmer reached the graveyard at all, hiding as it did behind its high railings and chained iron gates. An icy crust crept over rows of higgledy-piggledy gravestones; jutting, toppling and crumbling like scurvied teeth.

A bell in the tower clanged. A drunken fleshmonger staggering home in bloodied apron groped his way along the railings, grunting and trying unsuccessfully to whistle a tune. A horse's hooves clip-clopped over cobbles, pulling its clattering cart towards the slumbering city. An owl hooted from a desolate tree where frosty twigs poked through the mist, like clasping claws. Then silence. Deathly still. Nothing.

The first thud thumped through the night, as a spade struck mud. Two shadowy shapes stirred beneath a flickering lantern. One bent low to scrape at the ground.

'Keep digging,' he growled, 'And get that sack ready. It's a fresh mound. No headstone. Buried today, I shouldn't wonder.'

The other man put down the lantern. 'It might have the pox. Cover yer face.'

They pulled rags over their noses and tied them tightly behind their heads, before lifting their spades once more and stabbing them into the earth. Below the frozen surface, the soil was soft and loose – as a body had been buried only that morning.

A live body, as it turned out.

A spade came down with a crack. 'It's the coffin. We've got it.'

The lantern spilled its pale light into the hole.

'Ssh! Don't move. Keep still.'

'What's the matter?'

'I heard a noise. It sounded like the gate.'

They dived behind a slab, throwing a sack over their lantern. Its wick fizzed and the sack smouldered. A night watchman peered into the darkness, his beady eyes on the lookout for nocturnal body-snatchers. Fresh graves had recently been dug open and bodies taken away. Midnight robbers unscrewed gold rings from bony fingers inside coffins. But lately there was another prize. A body could fetch a good price if you knew where to sell it. Surgeons in the city would pay well for a human body to dissect in anatomy lessons. A young fresh corpse was ideal. No questions asked.

The watchman shone his lamp across the headstones before turning back to cross the cobbles, his footsteps swallowed by the night. The owl swooped silently, skimming a yew hedge before screeching from the tower, as the two men emerged in a swirl of cloudy breath. They dug the remaining soil from the coffin and scraped its rough wood bare. Neither heard the tapping from the other side of the lid. Instead, they held their breath as the axe swung above their heads and glinted in a drizzle of moonlight. The blade came down with a crack and split the lid in two. In the glow of the lantern, they glimpsed a face staring up at them. A white face smudged with soot – and eyes that stared up in horror… just as the moon peeped through the swirling mist.

Body-snatchers

—— *Chapter 2* ——

I couldn't believe what I saw when the lid above me smashed to pieces.

It was just as well I didn't see how closely the axe blade sliced by my nose. As I blinked up to the sky, four startled eyes stared back. I couldn't see who they belonged to, for a lantern's glare blinded my light-starved eyes. Suddenly cold air filled my lungs as I sat up and gasped out a steamy cloud. The two men screamed through the rags tied round their mouths. They dropped their shovels and ran behind a tomb, as an avalanche of mud slid into my lap. I now realised the awful truth that I wasn't being rescued at all. These men weren't friendly souls on an errand of mercy. Instead, they were robber rapscallions intent on skulduggery. What's more, I was still likely to be in mortal danger. As the saying goes: out of the cauldron and into the flame.

The lantern toppled from its pile of earth and struck me on the head, singeing my hair and knocking me back into a momentary trance.

As I rubbed my head and tried to sit upright, the spluttering lamp fell to my lap, licking blue flame around the discarded rose. A flickering glow curled up to my face, just as the robbers once more peered down.

'By heaven almighty, that be a sprite what's come to life, Horace. A will o' the wisp!'

'A ghostly child,' spluttered the other. 'A ghoul sent to haunt us, if ever there was.'

'What shall we do, Horace? Treat it with due respect and politely make our leave?'

'Nah – smack it on the 'ead with yer shovel.'

I reached up to pull myself to my feet, as they cowered behind a marble cross.

'Go on, Jack, throw the sack at it.'

The sack hit me and smashed open the lantern, dribbling burning oil into the coffin. The split lid suddenly ignited and instantly engulfed the sack in a ball of flame. I hurled it above my head in a burst of blazing light.

'It's an angel. A heavenly being in a cascade of divine radiance!'

'No, Jack. It's me sack going up in smoke.'

The plumper of the men, who wore a battered top hat, raised a stick as if to beat me, but his wiry partner, with a face like a frightened ferret's, seized the stick and whispered, 'Listen, Horace... that boy might be an angel. An angel of death, perhaps. It might be in our interests to befriend him – or he might smite us with one wave of his cherubic hand.'

'You might have a point, Jack. I fear the supernatural is in our midst and I'd hate to incur the wrath of some omnipotent force. Not as well as the wife.'

'Exactly my point. But, and here's my point more exactly... it could be to our considerable advantage if this risen corpse... angel... sprite... call him what you will... if he could be used for our financial gain. I know of a certain Gallimaufry

17

Garderobe who runs a travelling circus, with a freak show. People would pay us handsomely to come to be blessed by this resurrected cadaver. He may well possess healing powers and properties, the like of which could transform mankind but, more to the point, he could make you and me a sizeable fortune, if you get me drift.'

By this time, I was trying to clamber from my grave, weak as I was. With the sack now burnt out, I was back to shivering and feeling dizzy in the head. It was still a mystery to me as to why or how I came to be here in the first place but one thing I did know; I didn't want to get tangled with these two unsavoury characters. While they disappeared behind a tomb once more, engaged in hushed whispers which grew ever louder as they argued angrily as to what to do with me, I gained a foothold and, at last, a handhold. I was soon sprawled in the mud by their shovels but at least I'd escaped the grave. Now all I had to do was creep away and climb the huge iron gates, without the men noticing I'd gone. Easier said than done.

I crunched through a puddle crusted with a film of ice, numbing my bare feet. Moonlight shivered in its icy ripples. Hoping the men hadn't heard me, I began clambering up the iron gate. Despite my freezing limbs, I was still able to scramble nimbly enough – after all, I was used to shinnying up chimneys at the drop of a hat (or the whack of my master's stick). So, in a matter of seconds, I stood atop the high brick pillar beside the gate. It was then, as I turned to look back at the site of my burial, that I almost fell – outstretching my arms to regain my balance. That was when the men emerged and looked up. What they saw seemed to put them in a trance, for with outspread arms in a white shimmering shroud, it appeared I hovered like a phantom in mid-air. As the full moon shone behind my head, they thought they saw a halo of holy light about my face.

The larger man, who had previously seemed the more aggressive, dropped to his knees, clasped his hands and called up to me.

'Forgive us, oh holy one. We didn't mean you no harm. We'll swiftly shovel back this mud and return yer grave to its former glory. No one will be none the wiser and we'll be gone, sweet seraphim or cherubim or whatever celestial being of the 'eavenly 'ost yer 'appen to be.'

His scrawny friend nudged him. 'It might not speak English. Try Latin.'

'I don't know any Latin.'

'Then how about singing a hymn?'

'I don't know any 'ymns.'

'Then let me…' He cleared his throat and began chanting a warbling dirge.

'And though worms destroy this body, yet in my flesh will I see… er no… have mercy upon us, miserable offenders, we beseech thee….'

'Flesh? Offenders? Try something more holy!'

'I'm not used to anything holy – I'm a rat-catcher.'

'Then how about being an angel-catcher? If we could only get our hands on this flying seraph, we'd be blessed for life.'

'Look out, it's flying this way. It's swooping down to get us…'

Whether it was from cold or from the exertion of climbing so high in my weakened state, I tottered on my perch before passing out. In my faint, I felt myself fall. The last I remember was diving towards the two terrified faces – before all went black once more.

Crushing bones to climbing chimneys

⸺ *Chapter 3* ⸺

The unconscious mind does strange things. Mine shut out the horrors of the graveyard and of the hands that grabbed me, as it flicked open the pages of my story, fanning blurred images of how I came to be there in the first place. In a flutter of disconnected memories, I glimpsed faded pictures swirling up from the depths of my past. The first was of my father, whom I scarcely knew. In fact, there were only three things I ever knew about my life before I went to the workhouse. The first was that my father, Cornelius Catchpole, died of the dreaded smallpox plague that swept through the village where we lived. The matron of the workhouse told me I was about three years old at the time. The only other thing she let me know from my persistent questions was that he worked on the land some miles away and that he and I lived alone after my mother died giving birth to me. I never even knew her name. That often made me cry at bedtime, after each long day of crushing bones with a hammer. Hour after hour, day after day we had to break up the fleshmongers' carts of putrid carcasses into dust, to be carried away in sacks for spreading on the land.

Sometimes, in my dreams, I could still see my father's face. I'm sure it was a kind face, despite what they said about him. 'What sort of a man would mark his own child with such a hideous and barbaric tattoo?' As far as I was concerned, my tattoo of an Indian woman on my wrist was neither hideous nor barbaric. It made me feel special and was the only image I had to remind me of my father. I liked to think my parents had travelled the seas and explored the mystic East, where I might have been born in a golden palace. The priest who came to the workhouse to bury the dead told me disapprovingly that such marks on the wrist or fingers were eastern heathen superstitions to ward away illness. He insisted on scrubbing it off many times with a stiff bristle brush that tore my skin but I was always glad, once the scratches healed, that the little Indian lady reappeared, still smiling. Whoever she was, she was my only friend in all those long years at the dismal workhouse: Brickdyke Home for the Destitute. No one else had a cheerful face to talk to whenever they needed it. Nowhere else was a friendly face to be found – until the day I discovered in the most unlikely of places an exact copy of my tattoo's smiling features.

At eight years old, towards the end of 1801, I was apprenticed to Artimus Groundling, a mean and cruel chimney sweep. He came to the workhouse looking for a climbing boy and chose me from a long line of children. He looked in our ears, prodded our chests, examined our teeth and inspected our hair for lice. He grunted when he came to me, 'I'll have this one. I'll pay one guinea to the master of the workhouse for him, though I reckon I should get paid for taking the little beggar off his hands. It don't look like he needs much feeding and he's puny enough to fit up the narrowest flues. I don't want another one like the last. He got stuck in a zigzag and I had to burn him out but he still wouldn't shift. They say he's still up there and comin' down bit by bit when the odd blackened bone tumbles down.'

What few pennies I earned him from the sooty flues of filthy factories and grand houses, Artimus Groundling squandered in the gin palaces of the city. His body reeked of gin and soot, a sickly combination that kippered the lungs and pickled the mind. He would bark up at me from the hearths as I blindly groped my way above. 'Get higher, Cephas Catchpole, you workhouse ragamuffin. Scrub and brush or we starve. Just remember I saved you from a life of crushing bones. I'll crush your bones if you don't get up and scrape it clean.'

I slept on my master's floor under a sooty blanket and each morning, long before it was light, I had to walk the streets in bare feet crying 'Wee-eep! Wee-eep!'. Carrying my sack of soot and brushes, I was always tired and sore – and, of course, hungry. After all, if I was allowed to put on weight, I'd be unable to wriggle up and round those sooty tunnels.

Just sometimes, when working in the chimneys of grand country houses, a kind parlour maid might give me a drink or crust, but more often than not I'd be shouted at by housekeepers and treated worse than an ill-behaved dog.

Whether drunk or sober, Artimus Groundling always shouted at me. I don't think he could ever whisper or speak without snarling. His soot-wrinkled, gin-sodden face forever erupted in bubbling boils that he made me bathe before bed with rags dipped in scalding water. He insisted I apply steaming bread poultices to his neck, while he squealed like a trapped pig. He'd lash out at me if the boil burst, as if it was my fault. Then afterwards, when I'd carefully dabbed at the bloody pus, he'd splash it with gin and shake my hand for a job well done. Those were the only times he was civil to me but they didn't last. He found it difficult to be courteous to anyone and constantly moaned at his lack of success in 'catching a good woman'. I think that may have had a lot to do with his foul breath, a mix of gin and onions. He was of the firm belief that a diet of onions would purify his blood and keep the boils at bay. They clearly didn't but instead kept all women away. Nonetheless he insisted on eating raw onions for supper and breakfast – which meant I had to, too. No doubt my breath was equally odorous.

Master Groundling, as I had to call him, always wore a grubby top hat and a long black coat, even in summer. The soles of his boots were threadbare and, apart from a new pair of fingerless gloves that his sister knitted for him each Christmas, his appearance never changed. Nor did mine, come to that, for my sooty clothes were only scrubbed every few months, just like me. It was a thoroughly miserable eighteen months I spent as a chimney sweep, and a great disappointment for I'd been so desperate to learn a trade and escape the workhouse. When I was chosen from that long line of children, I'd felt so pleased. My father, I thought, would have been proud of me, just as my Indian guardian on my wrist must have been. But soon my soot-filled lungs, blackened knees, sore feet and scabby elbows caused constant discomfort and I longed to return to Brickdyke workhouse. I planned to run away on the day we worked in a country house miles from town. I would run off into the woods when Master Groundling chewed his onion lunch and swigged his gin. But in the end I didn't have to. For that was the day my life went from bad to worse… and it changed forever.

Brimstone House

—— Chapter 4 ——

The house was large and rambling, standing proudly in rolling countryside. We walked up the long drive in the early morning sunshine, birds calling from the woods where frosted branches had yet to sprout into leaf. I filled my lungs with clean air and felt the sun's rays on my face. I made the most of it, for I looked up at the towering chimneys that I was shortly to be squashed inside, squeezing my way up to a chink of sky and gasping for just a breath of fresh air. This was the delightful home, I was constantly being reminded, of the famous Doctor Mordecai Brimstone.

'Make sure you mind your p's and q's. If the good doctor is at home…' Master Groundling growled, 'I don't want to lose this customer. He works at the Gryme Street Hospital and he's a dab hand at lancing boils and I've a cracker coming on my rear. Instead of him paying for my service with cash, I shall ask him to bleed me. I'll get no money but at least I'll be able to sit down to munch my onions. It'll just mean I can't afford to buy bread this week so you'll have no supper. Unlucky.'

We went around to the back of the house where the housekeeper was beating a mat with a brush. 'Ah, it's you,' she said. 'The dust sheets are laid out in the parlour but heaven help you if a speck of dirt gets anywhere. Believe you me, I'll soon spot one bit of soot even on a piece of coal in the dark with me eyes shut. I've got eyes like a hawk, I have. That's what comes of all these years of having to see for two. And I'm not so keen at what I see right now. I don't like the looks of that little rat,' she pointed at me with her brush. 'If he touches anything he shouldn't, he'll get this brush round his ear and no mistake. I know where everything is and nothing must get out of place. The doctor is most particular and I'll be watching yer every move. You'd better not disturb her ladyship when she's up. I don't even want her to know you're here.'

'And how is the good lady?' Master Groundling asked with a smarminess I'd never heard before. We all knew his concern wasn't genuine.

'Much the same,' the woman said, bustling past us and through the door. 'Never complains.'

Although I had seen inside large houses before when taken to scramble up their chimneys, this was grander than all of them. There were enormous paintings hanging on every wall, of ladies wearing gowns or of ships with billowing sails, all in ornate gold frames. Polished furniture shone in rich dark browns as the sun streamed in through enormous windows surrounded by plush velvet curtains tied with corded tassels. I couldn't believe that anyone could own all of this. As if reading my thoughts, and doubtless having similar himself, Master Groundling tried to whisper, 'Wealthy people pay the doctor a fortune to keep them safe from the pox. He sells them his magic mixtures.'

The woman appeared behind us as we peered into the dining room. 'And why shouldn't he? Seeing as what the pox did to her ladyship, he deserves every penny, Groundling.'

'But of course, Mrs Quilter,' he answered awkwardly. 'Now where would you like us to start?'

The first chimney I had to climb rose from behind a cooking range in a back kitchen. Master Groundling unscrewed a section of pipe and I had to squeeze inside, wriggling through a very tight fit into the pitch black. Then, like a mole, I nuzzled blindly upwards through layers of ash and soot. Tar was encrusted on the brickwork beyond so I had to chip at it with a hammer and chisel, while Master Groundling kept shouting up at me not to make a noise, even though he was making far more than me. He clanged his spanner against the metal piping and the clatter rattled up past me and echoed around the chimney stack far above. As I climbed higher and the chimney narrowed, it was joined by flues coming up from other chimneys in other rooms. A constant sooty draft rushed past me to be sucked out the chimney pot somewhere above. It was as I was climbing round one twisting passage that I heard a sound drifting along it. By feeling my way through the solid blackness, I lowered my ear into the vent. It was the sound of someone weeping – haunting sobs and stifled crying. I remained very still for some minutes, listening to the ghostly wailing drifting up from somewhere below. I wasn't sure what to do but somehow I was slowly being drawn towards it. I felt I had to help whoever was in distress so I began clambering inside another chimney.

It was as I was wriggling round a tight bend that I dislodged a loose brick. It came away in my hand and clattered into the grate below. The wailing immediately stopped and I froze. In a gap behind where the brick had been, my fingers touched what I thought to be a stone jar with a stopper in the top. I couldn't see what it was but I thought the owner of the house might be grateful if I'd found something lost – so I tucked it inside my shirt and continued lowering myself further. As my feet dangled down into the empty fireplace, I was startled by a shrill scream. In a cloud of soot, I landed in the hearth and peered out into the room. A young girl in a green satin dress was sitting in a chair, clutching a rag doll and staring at me in petrified silence. Her dark curls tumbled over her shoulders.

'Don't be alarmed,' I said, taking a step forward, although I was probably more frightened, in case she'd scream again and bring Mrs Quilter with her dreaded brush.

'I heard someone crying…' I stuttered. 'Do you need help?'

She sat speechless, her face very pale and her eyes the deepest green, matching her dress. The way she stared unnerved me so I began backing away towards the chimney. I took the stone jar from under my shirt, to leave it on the mantelpiece before making a hasty exit. It was then she suddenly began shaking, screwing up her face, kicking her legs and squealing. I turned to face the fireplace to get out of there fast when I found myself face to face with a familiar smile. I was startled, to say the least. For there, on the stone jar on the mantelpiece was the face of the very same Indian woman tattooed on my wrist. Being unable to read, I had no idea what the words said under her smiling face. I was so stunned that I failed to notice the girl take a few steps towards me, before making another terrible noise. It was only then I realised that she was laughing. She was helpless with giggles and I was clearly the cause. Her rag doll landed at my feet as I tried to retreat up the chimney.

'I can't decide if you're the Soot Elf or a monkey escaped from the circus,' she chuckled, before stretching out her hand. 'Don't run away. At first you frightened me but you're the chimney boy, aren't you? They told me I might hear you clattering about up there. But I didn't think I'd actually see you! You just look so funny… and when you took that pot thing out of your shirt… what is it, anyway?'

I took a step forward and tried to be as polite as Master Groundling threatened me to be. 'I'm sorry to disturb you,' I began, 'but I thought you sounded very upset.'

'That was me crying,' she said, very matter-of-fact. 'I sit in this room and cry a lot. I hate it in here. I'm not allowed out until Mama gets up. Father locks me in. I so want to run and play outside but I have to do my lessons here by myself. My governess comes each afternoon before I'm sent back in here and locked up again. I'm twelve years old and I've never met another child. You're the first. And that's my horrible life. I can't help crying, you see.'

I was lost for words and could only ask, 'Why?'

'Why does he lock me away? To protect me. It's to stop me ending up like Mama. That's a painting of her.' She pointed to a small picture on the wall.

'She was beautiful then. She won't let me look at her face now and always wears a veil. Why are you staring at the pot you put on the shelf?'

'I found it up the chimney,' I said, and the rest gushed out all of a sudden. 'My name's Cephas Catchpole and I'm ten. My parents are dead and I've got my guardian on my wrist, look. I don't know who she is but I've just found her on that pot. Can you tell me what it says?'

I was so keen to know as I'd never known who 'My Lady', as I called her, could be.

'You poor thing,' she said. 'Now I feel bad for crying so much.' She looked at the stone jar with the stopper in the top. 'I can't really read it. It doesn't make sense. I think it must be a foreign name or something.' She sounded out the letters before saying slowly, '*Sitala Mata*'.

I was none the wiser. How I'd hoped that I might find out something about 'My Lady'.

'Come over to the window,' the girl said. 'Look down to the garden. Do you see that tree with sacks over the branches to protect them from frost? That's a dragon flower tree that my father brought back from India. There's a face scratched on its trunk just like that Indian lady. I would show you if they'd let me out. Mind you, I'll get into trouble if they find out I've let you in my room. They'd have it filled with flowers in case you've brought smells and disease. Can you smell those flowers in the vase? My father insists I keep the room smelling sweet to make sure no bad air gets to me and makes me ill. He makes his gardener bring flowers from the glasshouse every day. Look, roses in March!'

Despite the grand surroundings and lovely room in which she was imprisoned, I felt sorry for the girl. Her sad green eyes had no life or sparkle. Even though my life had often been miserable, I'd always had the company of others. And even though I never knew my father, I always thought of him warmly. The girl showed no such feelings when she spoke of her father.

'What's your name?' I asked.

'Edith. Edith Brimstone.'

'Aren't you pleased to have a doctor for a father?'

It was as though I'd just lit a firework. There was no stopping her now.

'I hate him. All he thinks about is smallpox and of going down in history for finding a cure and getting richer. It doesn't seem to matter how many people he kills or maims, so long as people give him a lot of money to inoculate them. And the thing is, he takes their money even though they may die. He knows his treatment is such a risk. Look what it did to Mama. And if he's so good, why won't he risk inoculating me? Instead I have to be wrapped up, locked away and never allowed to meet people. Do you know anything about smallpox?'

'Not much,' I said. 'I know it killed my father.'

'Exactly, it's often deadly. But once you get it and survive, you don't get it again. So my father spends all his time collecting the pus and scabs from smallpox victims so he can rub them into the arms of others to inoculate them. But more often than not it goes wrong. Mama nearly died and it blinded her. Her face is so badly scarred she won't let me look at her ever again. He won't let her touch me, let alone hold me in her arms.' Tears welled in her eyes.

'But he keeps on rubbing smallpox into people even though he's heard that another doctor has come up with a much safer treatment. I don't really understand it but I just know I want to get away from here.' She turned towards the door at the sound of a key rattling in the lock. 'Quick – someone's coming… you must go. Please come back and see me. I like you. I'll whistle up the chimney when it's safe to come back.'

I was already darting back to the fireplace when the door began to open. I hurled myself into the hearth, reached up to grip the sooty bricks and pulled myself up into the darkness. My feet dangled as I heard Edith shouting, 'Hurry… hurry…' followed by a man's voice that bellowed around the room and rose up the chimney.

'Who are you talking to?' I heard him shout. 'What is going on in here?'

'Nothing, father…'

But I wasn't ready for the next sound. It was an almighty scream that crashed around my ears and seemed to shake the whole chimney. 'What is that doing there? How did you get it?'

Edith was sobbing again. 'It's a pot, father. That's all. It came down the chimney.'

'You stupid girl. Keep away from it. Don't you dare touch it.' The next words were for me and for me alone – as he put his head into the fireplace and shouted up angrily.

'Whoever you are… I'm going to catch you and thrash the innards and entrails out of you. And if you don't believe me… just wait till we light fires in all the grates throughout the house. I'll soon smoke you out like trapped vermin. You will be consumed by flames and destroyed…'

The darkened room

—— *Chapter 5* ——

There was nowhere to hide. At least, there was nowhere to hide from smoke. For although I was still well-hidden from those who wanted to catch me and tear me apart, the fires they lit in almost every hearth throughout the house were quickly seeking me out. I clung on inside a narrow flue, as woodsmoke curled around me. Soon I'd be forced into the open if I ever wanted to breathe again. My lungs burned with the acrid fumes and my flesh scorched from the searing heat, as I hung like a cured ham in the choking blackness. My eyes smarted so much that I could do nothing but squirm and slowly shrivel. Like a salted slug, I shrank into a lifeless husk, barely able to move. Whichever tunnel or side-chimney I considered trying to climb up or down, shouts and yells swirled in each, carried in the twisting smoke and spiralling sparks.

'Just you wait till I gets me hands on yer, ungrateful wretch,' Master Groundling cried with a rage, for I'd dared to disgrace him in front of those he longed to impress. That was an unforgivable sin and my punishment was guaranteed. Not that I understood what all the fuss was about. From another vent came the squeals and shrieks of Mrs Quilter, who was equally outraged and seemed to be rushing around in a frenzy as if I'd committed the crime of the century.

'I told you he was nothing but a rat. I'll beat him to a pulp as soon as we flush him out. I've got a brush with extra sharp wire bristles. They'll soon rip his backside to shreds and no mistake.'

But far more sinister was the determined promise from Doctor Brimstone, interrupted by the pleading sobs of his daughter Edith. He spoke with a dangerously soft voice that was far more menacing, as its threatening tone cut right through the spits and crackles of burning kindling.

'If that urchin has fouled the air of my house, then he must be purified with fire itself...'

So I tried again to clamber blindly through tunnels clogged with sooty cinders in the hope of finding just a tiny refuge where smoke and singeing sparks couldn't reach me. As I wriggled along a narrow flue that squashed up my shoulders right into my neck, I suddenly felt cold air fanning my cheek where a hollow passage fell away into the blackness below. It seemed to be a chimney coming up from another room somewhere beneath me – and it was miraculously smoke-free. As soon as I descended into it I could at last breathe again. An updraft cooled my legs and I sucked in the beautiful air with rasps of relief. It took a long time for my body to gain any strength and for my eyes to stop streaming. I tried to open them and as I blinked through sooty tears, I became aware of a grey square of light emerging in the blackness below. It was presumably a fireplace down there that had yet to be ignited, although I guessed it was only a matter of time before smoke and flames would be raging from there as well. Desperate to escape my sulphurous prison, I descended into the unknown space. I slowly lowered myself, my knees bent up to my chest and my feet pressed against the coal-tarred bricks that also tore the skin on my back. The shouts and squeals of my pursuers still echoed above, through all the connecting chimneys. It was as if the hunters, like terriers trying to chase out a rabbit from its burrow, would stop at nothing to seize their prey.

At last I stood in an empty fireplace, relieved to feel solid ground under my feet and have space to un-hunch my aching body. I gingerly stooped to peer out into the gloomy room beyond. A decorated silk screen stood in the hearth to hide the fireplace, so I felt sure no one had seen me. I was in a bedroom with its heavy curtains closed and, as I peeped over the screen, a four-poster bed slowly took shape in the semi-darkness. Beside it on a mat was a washing bowl and jug, with towels draped on a stand. I was suddenly aware of someone sitting in a rocking chair near the window, slowly rocking to and fro. It was a woman in white – in a full nightgown to her ankles, wearing a mobcap, a shawl around her shoulders and woolly socks on her feet. But the room was too dark to see her face. I ducked behind the screen and prayed she hadn't seen me. I just didn't have the strength to clamber up the chimney again, back into the evil smoke and those terrifying tunnels. Much as I wanted to cough and stretch, I stayed very still, listening for the woman's breathing. If she was asleep, there was at least some chance of escaping from her room unseen. But suddenly I heard a faint chuckle that chilled me to the bone.

'I know you're there,' she whispered hoarsely. 'It's no use hiding.'

I daren't move. My stomach churned as I knew I'd be beaten or worse.

'Have you lost your tongue?' She spoke softly, almost sadly.

I slowly stood upright, to peer above the screen, but I could no longer see movement from the chair. I heard a door slam somewhere in the house, followed by the thunder of running feet on stairs. Voices called somewhere beyond.

'At first I thought you were a jackdaw. They often flap about in the chimneys,' she said, with another chuckle. 'But you're no jackdaw. So now I have to make a difficult choice. Unless you speak to me soon I'm afraid it could be a choice for the worse. If you don't tell me who you are I might do the wrong thing. Tell me and I'll decide what to do.'

I stood and waited, not knowing whether to speak or whether to make a dash to the door, even though there were now louder shouts and thuds just outside.

'It's no use trying to creep away,' she went on. 'That door is locked from the outside. So you see, we're both prisoners, aren't we? You can step a little nearer. I won't hurt you, you know.'

I stepped out into the room, the floor creaking beneath me, and I tried to catch a glimpse of the woman's face but it was covered by what looked like a mask. Her hands were clenched in white gloves and I couldn't tell what she looked like or how old she was.

'You probably wonder why I look so strange. Don't be frightened. I don't want to hurt you – not like the others out there want to. I've been listening to all their rants. They get so excited about such silly things. I can tell you're just a child. I've learned to recognise footsteps. Yours are very tiny so there can't be much to you. Do tell me your name.'

I still couldn't move and my tongue felt glued to the roof of my smoky mouth.

'If you don't hurry up they'll find you in here,' she said with greater urgency.

I suddenly blurted, 'My name's Cephas.'

'Ah, just as I thought. A young boy. So now I must decide what to do with you.'

'I'm the chimney boy and for some reason I've upset them all,' I said.

'So I gather. I've heard some of the goings-on. How old are you, Cephas?'

'Ten, madam.'

'Poor boy. Fancy having to climb up those filthy chimneys at your age. I wouldn't allow such things but sadly I no longer have any say in the running of the house. I'm blind, you see, and that seems to make them think I'm incapable and must be kept out of sight and not be listened to. I can't even talk to my daughter for more than a few minutes each day in case either of us catches something from the other. None of us is free.' She sighed sadly.

'I've just met Edith,' I said. 'She's very friendly. But I shouldn't have spoken to her. That's why I'm in trouble.' I could hear Master Groundling shouting nearby.

'Poor Cephas. Is that man with the loud voice your father?'

'No. He's my master. I don't have a father. Nor a mother.'

'Does that mean you have no surname?'

'Yes. It's Catchpole. I'm Cephas Catchpole.'

It was just as if a bee had flown into the room and stung the woman. Until then she'd been very still but all at once she twitched her hands and seemed to jump before shuffling in the chair, which began jerking back and forth.

'Do you know your father's first name?' she asked in a whisper.

'Yes,' I said. 'He was Cornelius Catchpole.'

The chair stopped rocking and the woman sat frozen like a statue before slowly leaning forward to speak secretively, the chair tilting almost to the point of tipping over. 'You must go,' she snapped. 'You must go and never come back. Climb out of the window. They won't see you scrambling down the pipe. Be careful, it's a long drop.' She reached out and tugged at one of the curtains, which slid towards her as a gash of sunlight slashed across the room. I screwed up my eyes and groped my way towards the window.

'Thank you for helping me,' I said, as my hands tugged at the casement window.

'The same manners,' she murmured. 'Polite even in adversity.'

I didn't understand what she meant, as I tried unsuccessfully to lift the heavy casement.

'Take my hand,' she said. 'Place it on the frame so I can help you. It often gets stuck.'

I stretched out my arm and touched her gloved hand. Although her face was covered, I could see the skin around her mouth and chin was pitted with a rash of little craters. Her neck was smothered with unsightly bumps and lumpy clusters.

'I'm sorry about your illness,' I said, not knowing what to say. 'And I'm sorry about my hand but I'm very dirty you see and…' As I placed her hand on the window frame, I was aware that she was crying.

'No one has ever touched me like that before. So gentle, so kind. Normally they grab me by the elbow and push me around like some old bag of dirty washing to be kept at arm's length. That's if anyone touches me at all. I've never been allowed to hold my own daughter. That's what comes of being claimed by the speckled monster. Forever ugly and assumed to be deadly.'

47

'You mean the smallpox?' I said.

'The scourge. Sometimes called "the red death" or "the great fire". It comes in so many different guises. Beware of Variola Major, the one that kills or disfigures. That's what I had seven years ago. It finally caught up with me and then took over the whole house.'

'It killed my father,' I told her.

'The same epidemic. It caught a lot of us without warning. And now it's taken over my husband's entire life. It's the enemy he has to destroy at all cost – and anything unclean that might harbour it. Dirt is the curse… and earth and soot and nasty smells… and grubby little chimney boys...'

I was puzzled by something she'd said and was about to ask an important question when a key rattled in the door behind us.

'Quick,' she said with increased urgency. 'We must lift the window together…'

The casement rose slightly and juddered before jamming. However much we both pushed and shoved, it just wouldn't shift any more. I heard the handle of the door turning.

'I can just squeeze through the gap,' I said, wriggling under the frame that I'd smothered in grubby handprints.

'Then do so, quickly. I'll draw the curtains back across and you must hurry down the drainpipe. Run across the lawn into the woods before they set the dogs after you. Good luck.'

The curtains swished shut behind me as I scrambled out into the cool sunlight and clung to a ledge. A beautiful garden of shrubs and unusual trees stretched beneath me, but there was no time to admire the view. Raised voices were already dangerously close behind, as I stretched out to reach a drainpipe. I grabbed hold of it and clung on tightly, with my feet still on the windowsill. The curtains ripped open again, the window clattered up with a roar and Doctor Brimstone's face screamed just a few feet away. All I could see was his bald head, tufts of ginger hair sprouting from his nostrils and a pair of wire-rimmed spectacles perched just above them. I could hear his wife behind him, her own voice now much louder as she tried unsuccessfully to reason with him. He brushed her aside, leaned out further through the open window and lunged at me. His hand grabbed my ankle and pulled violently as he spat and snarled, his nose-hair quivering. I squealed as my hands slipped from the drainpipe.

All at once I lost my grip, just as he lost his grip on my ankle… and I fell like a stone, headfirst to the brick path below.

Lifeless

—— *Chapter 6* ——

The girl in the locked room heard everything.

'Looks like he's dead.'

'I'm not surprised after a fall like that. He isn't moving.' The doctor placed a finger to the neck.

Artimus Groundling's retort tumbled through the gardens, scattering birds like musket fire. 'He took me a good while to train, you know. I'll have to get another workhouse boy now. More expense. A few shillings will cover only part of my inconvenience.'

'Your inconvenience? What about the mess you've caused because of this filthy reprobate? I should never have hired you. If my daughter falls sick from his filth, I will have you thrown into gaol and transported. It would have been far preferable if I'd done the same as previous years by releasing a few chickens down the chimneys. They flap and clean out the soot far better than your incompetent methods – and at least there's a feast afterwards. When the fires are lit, the birds land in the dining room already cooked. There's no flesh on this chimney boy worth the roasting.'

Artimus Groundling shuffled his feet. 'So can't I persuade you to take a look at my rear end?'

'Are you mad?'

'No – just a bit sore. Boils. A peep, that's all. I've got a bulbous monster that needs lancing. A proper throbber. It won't take you long to give it a quick squeeze and a prod with a red-hot needle.'

'You'll never afford my fees.'

Mrs Quilter poked her head out of the scullery door. 'I've got a bucket of cold water, Doctor. Shall I throw it over the rat-boy?'

'If you must.'

The woman waddled towards them as water sloshed from her bucket and slapped across the path in huge slopping splatters. She poured what remained over the patient, as well as over the shoes of the two men.

'I think I heard him groan.' Artimus Groundling leaned forward, screwing up his nose as he looked down at the sprawled body.

'If I have to treat him, you will have to pay.' The doctor was more concerned with wiping his shoes on a lavender bush.

'In that case, he must be dead.'

'I will provide one measure of laudanum at no cost, but thereafter, all treatment will be charged at normal rates.'

'Very well. I'll wash the measure down his throat with a few swigs of my cheapest gin. That should sort him out. Kill or cure, eh? And while the boy's either reviving or expiring, would it be in order for me to lower my trousers right here, doctor?'

'Mister Groundling!' Mrs Quilter gasped as she dropped the bucket with such a clatter that the boy's eyelids fluttered. 'You'll do no such thing anywhere near my kitchen. I won't have my serving girls and parlour maids exposed to such a disgusting countenance. You'll curdle the junket in my jug.'

'I only wish for the doctor to attend my boil, Mrs Quilter.'

'That's as maybe. Boil or no boil, a rear is a rear. Such sights are not for the faint of heart or delicate custards in my kitchen.'

'I think I saw the boy stir.' Doctor Brimstone reached for a hip flask, unscrewed the top delicately, and slowly poured a dark liquid between the patient's mauve lips.

'Not that the wretch deserves an ounce of my attention,' he muttered.

'You are just too kind, Doctor Brimstone. Nothing short of a saint.' Mrs Quilter clutched her rattling bucket and waddled back inside the house, taking one last long look at Artimus Groundling, to check that his trousers were still firmly belted. When his hands fumbled under his coat, she was about to scream at him but he produced a flask of his own, so she tutted and stepped indoors.

Not being familiar with pouring gin down the throats of others, Artimus Groundling was less accomplished than the doctor at administering his medicine. The gin slurped over the patient's chin before a trickle eventually spluttered down his throat with a gurgle. Both men looked down disdainfully at the drenched, lifeless specimen, as Mrs Quilter returned with a woollen rug smothered in dog hairs and all manner of stains.

'He don't deserve it but he can borrow the dog's blanket to keep out the chill. It's just been sick on it but it's more than good enough for the wretch.' She hurled it down and a cloud of dancing dog hairs drifted over the shrubbery.

Doctor Brimstone took a watch from his breast pocket, attached on a silver chain. He clipped open its cover, flashing sunlight across his spectacles, pondered for a moment then snapped it shut. 'I need to go,' he said. 'I have business to attend to. You, Groundling, get inside and clean up any dirt you and that vermin of yours made in my house. I shall inspect everything on my return and adjust the price of the operation accordingly.'

'Of my boil?'

'Not your boil, fool. Your festering, putrid lump has nothing to do with it, man. Only in as far as it is your rear that will receive a firm kicking if I am not entirely satisfied with the state in which you leave my property. I hope I make myself clear. As for the chimney-rat at our feet, just leave him be until he either awakes or expires. There are wooden boxes in one of my sheds suitable for dispatching the body. Should further treatment be necessary, I will remind you that my fees are far beyond your ability to pay. Either way, you are left somewhat inconvenienced. And as for the boil on the buttock, it is at times like this you might ponder that it pays to have sweeter breath and closer friends who might be prevailed upon to assist with your more intimate concerns.' He turned with a click of his heels and left Artimus Groundling to consider the advice and to reflect upon his predicament.

Edith Brimstone sneaked out of the house as the sun was sinking behind the woods. With her father still at the hospital, her mother being led by Mrs Quilter around the glasshouse, and her governess having just left, there were a few minutes of freedom before she would be locked in her room once more. While the strange man in the long black coat continued to sweep around the hearths throughout the house and the other staff were busy preparing dinner, there was time at last for her to discover for herself the scene of the commotion she'd heard and partially seen from her room.

When she turned the corner of the house, Edith gasped. At first, she thought it was one of the dogs stretched on the path and covered in a blanket. But as she approached, she saw a boy lying on his back, half under a lavender bush, with his head to one side and his eyes closed. She stooped beside him and gingerly reached out to touch his blackened face and matted hair. Tears spilled down her cheeks as she whispered, 'Cephas, what have they done to you. I'm so sorry…'

'Don't you dare touch him!' Mrs Quilter stood over her, waving a small bunch of primroses.

'Quickly sniff these to cleanse your breath of his foul odours and step right away from him.'

Edith blinked across to where her mother sat on a bench in the dying sun. 'Mama, they've killed him.'

Her mother sat up. 'Where, my love? Not Cephas? I assumed he'd escaped. Mrs Quilter, come and fetch me. Take me to him.'

'But madam, he was a wicked boy to disobey the doctor. He made a sooty mess in both your chambers and he had the audacity to enter each of them against orders.'

'It wasn't just that,' Edith sobbed. 'He found a jar hidden up the chimney and when father saw it, he went into a rage. It wasn't Cephas's fault. I liked him. He made me laugh… for once.'

'His laughing days are done,' Mrs Quilter said coldly. 'The fact is, he's a bad 'un. Any child encrusted in filth is a risk to all of us. I've long believed soot hastens the pox, feeds the fever and stirs the monster. Keep well away from that unclean corpse.'

'No, Mrs Quilter.' Edith's mother held her by the arm. 'He's Cephas Catchpole.'

'Catchpole?'

'Yes.'

'Holy Moses! Not…. Catchpole.'

'Exactly, Mrs Quilter. But you mustn't tell my husband. None of us must. It has to remain a secret.'

Edith ran, still sobbing, into the house. Her mother sighed. 'I'm afraid it's a sad day that the poor boy came to grief at this place and in such a manner. A final twist of fate and I fear each of us is partly to blame for his untimely end.'

Mrs Quilter led her away with a brisk, 'Then we must go inside, madam and leave the child in peace. I will instruct the sweep to come out and make good the body before nightfall. There is already quite a chill in the air.'

The moon was already rising in a clear sky by the time Artimus Groundling had acquired a hammer, nails and a wooden box of the appropriate size. He stood in the moonlight, swigging his gin when Doctor Brimstone returned.

'Still here, man? There's a handcart in one of the sheds for you to remove the corpse. Make sure you return it by daylight.'

'What do you suggest I do with the deceased, doctor?'

'Do with it as you will. If it were of a decent size, I would have use of it at the hospital. I doubt if this specimen's puny innards are worth slicing up for anatomy lessons. I like plump livers and lungs to slap on the tray for training doctors to prod, poke and chop into chunky lumps.'

All colour drained from Groundling's sickly face as his hand clutched his mouth. The doctor stooped to lift up the boy's arm to feel for a pulse. 'Throw it into the river for all I care.'

It was then he glanced down at the limp wrist in his hand. 'Ye gods, what is this? Is this some kind of trick you are trying to play on me, you villainous rapscallion?'

He dropped the arm and took a crimson silk handkerchief from the same pocket as his watch and dabbed feverishly at his bald brow. He staggered backwards and grasped a pillar to support himself.

'You seem somewhat vexed, doctor. Allow me to assist.' Groundling wiped the doctor's clammy face, its ginger tufts and blotchy cheeks, before poking the handkerchief clumsily back into the breast pocket. The doctor lunged forward and grabbed Groundling's coat collar.

'Was it you who inscribed that face on the boy's wrist in some roguish attempt to do further mischief? Such superstitions have no place here, do you understand? I've had enough of you and your knavish tricks. So just box up this dead wastrel and be gone.' He shoved him to one side, stamped his foot in a burst of flatulence, turned and swept indoors, tripping up the step and cursing loudly.

Artimus Groundling took another flask from inside his filthy coat and sat on the wooden box, carefully resting on one buttock to avoid squashing his boil, while taking regular swigs and staring up at the moon.

'I keep special sloe gin for moments like this, young Cephas. You've caused me great trouble today but I give you a toast with my finest brew to send you on your way. Think yerself lucky. Ten years old and you've escaped this cruel world. I don't know how long I've got left of trying to earn a crust… and growing me onions. But what's going to 'appen to me when I get old and sick? I've got nothin'. Nothin' in the world. You're well out of it, boy.'

He wiped a tear from his eye, oblivious to Edith standing behind him, holding a shirt and a flower.

'You must be upset,' she said softly.

He looked down at the body. 'I am, Cephas. You're too right.'

He stood and took another swig before staring down quizzically, then spluttering with shock as Edith tapped his shoulder.

'I've brought one of father's white shirts to put him in. Father doesn't know, of course. I want you to bury Cephas in something clean.'

She knelt beside the body and pulled the shirt over Cephas's head, sniffing as she did so.

As soon as the body lay in the box, Edith carefully arranged the shirt, smoothing out all the creases. She placed his arms across his chest and put the flower between his fingers; a single white rose.

'I've just said a little prayer,' she said. 'Where will he be buried?'

'Churchyard,' the chimney sweep continued, spluttering between swigs. 'There'll be no fuss. I know the gravedigger. He'll dispatch him fine for a glass of me brew and a pickled onion.'

'Then will you ask him to mark the grave with this?' She held a small cross made of twigs, tied together with blue ribbon. 'I made it from the dragon flower tree.'

Her name suddenly rang out behind them from somewhere inside the house. Her father's angry shouts echoed across the moonlit lawns. Staying remarkably composed and with all the dignity she could manage, Edith looked once more into the box before turning to walk swiftly indoors.

After trying many times to return the flask to his pocket, Artimus Groundling lifted the wooden lid from the path and slammed it on top of the box. He hammered it down securely with large iron nails, the crack of each hammer-blow reverberating through the night and bouncing off the distant trees. He sang tunelessly and mumbled words of remorse to the body inside. Then, after lifting the box onto a handcart, he began the long walk home – pausing every so often down the drive of Brimstone House for yet another swig and a bite of onion from his sooty pocket. The further he staggered, pulling the squeaky contraption in ever increasing zigzags, the louder his chuckle grew until, eventually, when the church tower came into view, he leant against the cart and guffawed.

'Nearly home, my lad. Yer final resting place is in sight. And what's more, it ain't been such a bad day after all. Not for some of us, eh?' He reached inside his coat, into one of his other deep pockets and pulled out a crimson silk handkerchief.

'Nice quality. It'll fetch me a good few coppers. But not as 'andsome as the biggest prize, eh?'

He lifted up, as delicately as his cold fingers could manage, a fine silver chain – on the end of which swung a shiny watch that glinted the moon.

'Thank you very much, Mordecai Brimstone!' He threw his head back and cackled before tumbling drunkenly back into the cart – to the unmistakable 'pop and squelch' of a rupturing swelling.

His howl, like a werewolf beneath the silver

moon, sailed over the rooftops and up to the stars beyond. He lay crying like a baby and drowning his sorrows for the best part of an hour. The boil had done its worst.

A grimy garret

—— Chapter 7 ——

ven before I opened my eyes, I knew I was in a strange place. I dreaded opening them at all, in case I was still buried underground inside a coffin. But from surrounding sounds, I sensed I was in a room, lying face-down and covered by a blanket of some sort. My head was resting on something soft with an unfamiliar smell, quite different from my usual waking sensations of soot, gin and onions. Instead of the normal mumbling,

snorting and belching from Master Groundling, I could hear snuffles and mewing. It was then, as my eyes blinked open, that I realised the smell was cats.

The room was dark but various shapes slowly emerged in the orange glow coming from the coals on a stove. Across the room on a windowsill, a single candle was stuck in a beer bottle at a precarious angle, dripping its wax into a twist of dribbling fingers. It spluttered its flickering light over a patchwork of windowpanes that were either cracked, covered with sacking patches or smeared with grime. The room's walls and ceiling were stained with dark blotches, veined with cracks or in places bare of plaster entirely, revealing wooden planks behind. On an upturned tea chest beside the stove were three pewter pots, half a loaf and a block of lard on a plate. A frying-pan hung by a string from a nail in the wall and beneath it, on a pile of sacks, lay a purring cat contentedly licking a litter of squeaking kittens.

As I struggled to sit up, I found I'd been lying on a thin straw-filled mattress on the bare floor and my blanket was a sack. The angled ceiling told me I was in an attic room and by the foot of my mattress was a hole in the floor through which poked the top of a ladder. I squinted at it, trying to make sense of a round shadow with a blinking fleck of light. It was only when I leaned forward and rubbed my eyes that I saw it was a boy's face and he was winking at me. Only his head and shoulders poked up through the floor and he rested his chin on his folded arms and grinned.

'Woke up then, Angel?'

I stared at him, not knowing what to say. After a long pause, he spoke again.

'Speak English? Lost yer tongue?'

'Who are you?' I asked, my words coming out in a strange croak.

'You sound more like a frog than an angel. Uncle Jack said you might have magic powers. Just what we need right now.'

'Who?'

'Uncle Jack. He dug you up but you scared him so much he took to the bottle as soon as he got you here. He's sleeping it off – snoring like a farrowing sow. I'm the only one awake – apart from you now.' The boy's cheeky face was fixed in a grin, but as far as I could see, his mouth had no teeth. His hair was closely cropped and his right eye continued to wink each time he spoke.

'So who are you?' I repeated.

'If you're a heavenly being, you should know. I'm Tooth Cutpurse.'

'Tooth?'

'Yeah, that's what they all calls me on account that me gums don't have none, except the one, that is. They've all been pulled. I've been called it for years. I'm about nine but no one knows when I was born exactly. No mother, see.'

'So do you live here?' I asked.

'When it suits. Uncle Jack ain't bad but it's that lot downstairs what's the problem. The Dalrymples on the ground floor. We sleep on the next floor and up here's where we eat.'

I knelt up on the mattress and was about to try standing.

'You have to watch where you tread up here,' he went on, 'what with what them cats leave all over. Stinks, don't it? But don't complain, 'cause you've got the warmest place. Do you eat? Me uncle said to fry a couple of sausages, if that's what angels like.'

'Sausages?' Artimus Groundling never fed me with meat so I'd long forgotten what they were like.

'Yeah. They're good. Makes a change to sausages from the fleshmonger who adds minced sewer rats

68

to his mixture. Her downstairs makes 'em from our own pig. We shared him till last week when' – Tooth mimed cutting his throat – 'we carved him up. Nice lot of dripping. I got the bladder for a ball. Do yer like bacon? There's a rasher or two. We're a bit short, otherwise. It's market day soon so I'll lift a few bits for yer dinner. That's if angels don't mind pilfered fare. Me uncle says the food I lift off the carts tastes better than anything you can buy. I think he's right.'

'Are you a thief?'

'Don't look so shocked. I bet you're no angel yerself. Oh yeah… I was forgetting…'

'Is it true I was buried in a coffin?' I asked.

'Yeah. What did yer die of?'

'I'm not sure. I think I fell out of a bedroom window but maybe that was a dream.' I'd lost all sense of time and what was real. Had I really met a girl called Edith and her blind mother or was it all a nightmare brought on by some strange fever?

'Never mind, Angel. You won't be able to fly from this window as you'll never get it open. It's not much of a place here but it's warm and the rent's cheap. Dalrymple brings back a shovel of coal most nights. He knows of a yard down by the canal. In the summer I sleep out in town and bag up the horse muck to earn a few coppers. Uncle Jack says I should put some in me boots to make me grow!'

The boy chatted on cheerfully about anything that came into his head. I couldn't help liking him, with his jolly toothless grin, playful winks and carefree shrugs. His manner was in many ways like an old man's as he didn't speak like a child at all, being the sort of boy I could never imagine crying or getting upset. Even when a shriek and the smash of pots ascended from below, making the cat spring with a hiss, scattering kittens like skittles, he nonchalantly shrugged his shoulders again. 'That's the Dalrymples having one of their family chats. They fight most nights. Like cats. It's enough to give us all kittens, ain't it, Turnip?'

'Turnip?'

'Yeah, I found her as a kitten in a sack of turnips by the docks. She's a fine ratter, ain't yer, Turnip? Course, 'er downstairs was all for skinnin' 'er for gloves but so far I've kept 'er hands off 'er!'

Despite further yells and thuds from below, the cat returned calmly to her sack, to be nuzzled once more by her squawking brood. Another voice called from below but this time the cat was totally unperturbed.

'Is that you, Tooth?'

The boy didn't look down but continued grinning at me. 'Yeah, Uncle Jack. Just chatting to Angel.

We're getting' on just fine, ain't we?'

'Yes,' I said. 'I think so.'

Tooth clambered up the ladder to sit cross-legged on the floor, so that his Uncle could poke his head up through the hole. He was a thin, wiry man with pointed features and beady eyes.

'He's not flown back up to heaven, then?'

He looked at me warily, without smiling, then continued seriously. 'I have to be perfect honest with yer, Angel, you're a bit of a mystery to me. I'm not sure what to do with yer but I have a strong feeling you could bring us... how shall we say... many blessin's.'

The boy chuckled and winked at both of us.

'The fact of the matter is,' the man went on, as he climbed up into the room and sat on the tea chest, 'we really need to have a little chat, you and me. My friend, Horace on the ground floor, as well as his troublesome missus, were all set for droppin' yer in the canal with a couple of slabs round yer

gullet. But I says to 'em, "Nah, 'old on, me friends."
That's not because I'm a saint or nothin' – it's just
that I can sense a miracle when it's staring me in the
face. So let me start by asking you a simple question,
my friend. Are you a mortal being?'

I didn't understand what he was asking me. 'Not
really,' I said, trying not to offend him.

'Just as I thought,' he went on. 'So tell me, Angel,
what is it you want of me?'

I looked down at my filthy, itching arms and felt
the stinging, sooty cuts in my back and I heard
myself saying, 'Is there any chance of a warm bath,
do you think?'

The boy whistled. 'Cor, strewth! He definitely
ain't normal!'

'They do say,' the man continued seriously, 'that
cleanliness is next to Godliness. Does that mean
if you get scrubbed up you'll be wingin' your way
back up to the Almighty?'

I didn't have a clue what he was saying and all
these riddles confused me even more.

'That depends,' I heard myself saying, though I
had no idea why I said it.

'I thought it might,' he said thoughtfully, and
he leaned very close and whispered, 'I think we're

goin' to get along just fine. Are you happy to stay here for a while, if I fetch the bath tub? And would you like a bite of supper, perchance? Tooth, fry up a few onions for our little friend.'

'Er… if you don't mind,' I said shyly, 'no more onions. But a sausage would be welcome.'

The boy shrieked with laughter, rolled backwards on the floor and kicked his feet in the air.

'Stone the crows! What a gent!'

The cat stretched and sighed, as if having another mouth to feed was the last straw.

Graverobbers and gravity

—— *Chapter 8* ——

 'tand there and don't move.' Horace Dalrymple hissed in my ear as he removed my blindfold and waited for a cloud to hide the moon. 'You create a fuss and you'll get a shovel round yer neck. If I 'ad my way, yer'd be back in yer box six feet down. I hate boys, especially angels.'

The graveyard stretched before us beyond the gates, with shadows darker than the devil's throat.

There wasn't a wisp of breeze and the frozen stillness gripped the night in its icy claws. It was past midnight and the silence hung over us like the cloak of the Grim Reaper himself.

'It's Jack's idea that you're a holy omen. It's my idea you're a waste of breath. If you get caught, you daren't squawk a word, you hear? You don't know where we live and that's how it stays. Your job tonight is to be lookout. If need be, lead the watchmen off into them trees so we make our escape. If any of us gets caught, just remember the gallows awaits us all. If you so much as put a foot wrong I'll cut yer throat, holy or not. Me wife says yer no holier than a vest.'

In many ways, it was his wife who frightened me more than anyone. She was always in a temper, with a savage tongue and the cruellest eyes the colour of rotting seaweed – with teeth to match. Her tangled hair, sprouting in tufts among the bald patches, was streaked with rust and her equally rusty eyebrows met in a bristly clump above a sneering nose. Most of the time her expression was as if she'd just sat on a hornet's nest, with a face that was constantly flushed and about to erupt in an explosion of magma. In fact, I wondered if magma from previous eruptions had solidified in crusty folds under her chin where rashes and scabs matched the colour of her hair. I couldn't help thinking her warty, puffed neck looked just like a toad's. She never spoke to me, or to anyone for that matter, without hurling insults or flying into a pointless rage.

'If I don't earn good money tonight,' Horace Dalrymple muttered as he scaled the huge graveyard gates, 'the missus will give me a right shouting. And if she gives me a shouting, I'll give you far worse.'

I knew the two men with their spades were intent on digging open graves but I had no idea why. 'What is it you hope to find?' I asked. 'Is there money hidden in one of the graves?'

'That's right, Angel,' Jack Cutpurse cackled. 'This wheelbarrow is for cartin' off a treasure chest of gold coins. Let's just put it this way, my boy. By day I catch rats and by night I catch somethin' else.'

I could only mutter, 'I would think you're more likely to catch cold!'

'Shut yer noise,' Horace hissed, lifting the wheelbarrow and sacks effortlessly over the gate with his brawny arms. 'Keep yer silence. All yer need to know is that I dig canals by day and dig for other things by night.'

'Worms for fishing?' I asked.

'Now they would be very plump worms here and there'd be many of 'em well-fed round these parts, eh, my lad?' Jack sniggered.

'I said shut yer row.' Horace flicked him with a sack and clenched his fist menacingly.

I'd been staying in their attic for a few days and, having been fed, washed and rested, I was already feeling much stronger. Tooth had leant me his jacket, scarf and gloves, so this time, without a large flapping shirt to snag the bars, I was able to clamber up the gates and over the other side in no time.

'Did you see that?' Horace said. 'He's no angel, he's a monkey in a waistcoat. He can climb faster than a squirrel with his tail afire!'

'Yeah,' Jack whispered. 'Just what I was thinkin'. I think we've struck gold with Angel. He's goin' to come in very useful, I shouldn't wonder. I told yer this angel were a godsend.'

'Sshshsh. No more sound. Follow me.' Horace lit a lantern that spluttered and popped as he put it carefully inside the barrow before leading the way through a maze of towering gravestones. Soon he stopped, held up the lantern to get his bearings then whispered, 'You, boy… stay here on your own. Don't take your eyes off that gate.'

'It's too dark for me to see it,' I said.

'Shut up and listen. Keep watch. If you see a light over there or hear the gate being opened, throw a stone up at the church roof. That will tell us to get out quick. If anyone sees you, run to the trees. Got it? Keep yerself hidden behind that statue of an angel – like yerself!'

Jack ruffled my hair with a 'Don't get up to any mischief now, Angel. Keep us safe, eh?'

As their feet crunched away between the graves, leaving me alone in the choking darkness, I felt my flesh creep. My stomach was writhing with icy worms. I was convinced dead fingers were clawing up through the earth, about to clasp around my throat. They would dig out my eyes and slowly squeeze the breath from my body. My tears spilled onto the crumbling stone angel that I desperately clung to, but I had to stifle my sobs in case I was heard by the men with spades… or by the waking dead.

Why was I here? Why did I have to cower on the frozen moss in this fearful place? Until that moment I'd foolishly thought my luck was getting better. How comforting to wake the last few mornings in a warm room, with the ever-cheery

Tooth, a friendly cat, a supply of sausages and no more chimneys to climb. For once I'd felt as if my life was clambering out of darkness, but suddenly, here in the numbing terror of the graveyard, I was in the middle of something I knew to be both dangerous and despicable. I was petrified like never before. Although I had no idea where my sense of right and wrong came from, I knew instinctively I was involved in sinister goings-on. Horrifying though it was just a few nights before to find myself buried in a coffin, this somehow felt worse. I was no longer an innocent victim but up to my ears in something evil. I was now daring to disturb the dead souls around me, all angrily stirring and about to seek revenge. I was sure I'd perish this time and I shivered with a fear and guilt I'd never known before.

My snivels grew into uncontrollable sobs that snatched away my breath, as I crouched gasping for air. I'd never had anyone to love, other than the faintest memory of my father, but right then I knew no one in the world loved me, either. It was only there, in the suffocating blackness of the churchyard that awful night, that I not only realised for the first time that it mattered to no one if I lived or died, but I also sensed how lonely, evil and wretched this world could be. Even though I'd always known I had nothing at all in the world, the dismal truth dawned on me by that hideous statue. When you've got nothing in the world, you've got nothing in the world to lose. Apart from your life, of course – and I now knew I was taking that risk. Surely life could never get any worse than this?

The ends of my fingers, poking out of Tooth's moth-eaten gloves, traced the letters carved into a marble plinth. I became mesmerised by the shapes and curves as I caressed the stone. My sobbing stopped as I felt a strange comfort in the sensation at my fingertips. For I knew I'd done this before. Something deep in my memory began to stir – of tracing letters into sand. I'd never been able to read, but all of a sudden I could hear a voice in my head saying sounds to match the shapes my fingers made. There in the darkness, as my finger followed a snaking line, I felt my mouth say 'sssss'. However did I know? The fear and panic of the last minutes suddenly lifted as I heard my father's voice making sounds in my head. For the first time, I realised he must have started teaching me to read. And what of that other voice that told me about right and wrong – was that his also? My tears didn't stop, but they were different now. No longer was I petrified, but I was strangely assured by that discovery in my moment of utter misery. I was sure, despite everything, my father was giving me the strength to survive.

I must have sat there deep in thought for a long while until the clouds parted and the moon cast its milky light over the church roof, spilling onto the headstones beside me. As I looked up at the tower and a nearby tomb, I realised this was the exact spot where I'd been buried a few nights before. A mound of loose earth marked the place, as well as a small cross made of twigs tied with blue ribbon. But that wasn't all. A single rose lay on the soil but it wasn't the wilting white rose that was buried with me. This was a fresh yellow rose. It was as I reached out to touch it, wondering how it got there, that I heard the clang of iron and rattle of chains. I looked up to see shadows moving at the gates. Men with lamps, sticks and growling dogs were entering the churchyard.

This was the moment I'd dreaded. Whatever I was meant to be doing here, these angry men had come to stop me. I clutched at the soil and hurled a clod of mud up at the church roof. It splattered over the tiles with hardly a sound so I grabbed a lump of brick and threw that. It cracked on the roof and rattled down into the guttering, making enough noise to wake the dead. Men began shouting excitedly and their dogs barked, yelping to be released from their ropes. I wasn't going to stay a sitting target and let them sniff me out so I stood and ran.

'Hey, did you hear that? Someone's over there!' The dogs sprang as the ropes were released from their necks. I knew I'd never reach the trees without being torn apart by the snarling jaws but there was nowhere to hide. In an instant I decided to do the only thing I could possibly do – I climbed. Luck was on my side for once, for the clouds had closed across the moon and the deepest darkness stretched like a widow's veil over the graves. I scrambled up the trunk of an enormous yew tree, groping my way up into its dense interior. Beneath me, jumping dogs were howling like a pack of savage wolves, snapping just inches from my feet. By the time their handlers arrived beneath the tree, I was high up in the branches and well-hidden from their lanterns' feeble flickers. My dark clothes melted into the deep shadows and I remained perfectly still in the hope they'd think the dogs had been mistaken.

'There's got to be someone up there. I say we come back with a ladder and grab him.'

'I'm happy to sit here all night if need be.'

The frenzied barking and whacking of sticks against the tree didn't stop so I instinctively climbed a few steps higher. Suddenly something hit my face with such a scream that I lost my balance and tumbled through the branches. Somehow I clung on, just as the screeching owl swooped from the tree, just skimming the heads beneath me. There were shouts and curses as the owl flapped up into another tree, pursued by the baying hounds.

'The stupid dogs – it's just an owl they saw. That's not what we're after, you fools! We won't find any resurrectionists about their sordid business now. The dead themselves will have fled.'

With my heart still pounding, I clung to the branch that had broken my fall, until the night fell silent once more. The iron gates clanged shut and the panting dogs yelped off into the distance. I slowly lowered myself to the ground and squatted beneath the tree, pondering what the world might hold in store for me next, when in the ghostly stillness, I heard a faint cry. A hoarse voice was feebly calling 'Angel!'

I stood and groped my way through gravestones and bushes, trying to find where the muffled cries were coming from. I daren't call back in case this was some kind of trap so I remained completely quiet.

'Angel!' The voice was much nearer now. I trod softly towards it, through loose soil that clung to my feet, seeming to grip my ankles like the groping hands I dreaded – when I hit my shins on the wheelbarrow. It was then, somewhere below me, I heard another cry. It seemed to be coming from a hole in the ground and for a split-second I saw a glowing ghostly hand clawing up through the earth. I stepped back in horror, stumbling over a spade. My worst fear was becoming real.

'Is someone there?' The croaking voice rose from the hole and I froze.

'Is that you, Angel? Help us. You've got to get us out.' I could now see a flickering light in the hole from where the hand still reached up with bloody fingers. I crawled through the mud and peered inside, dreading bony fingers were about to grip me by the throat. From what I was able to see, the hole was no bigger than a man's fist beside a huge stone slab lying flat on the ground. I could hear groaning coming from somewhere below. I lay on the slab and put my mouth to the hole, unsure of what to do or say. 'Is that you, Uncle Jack?'

Immediately a voice called back. 'Praise the Lord! It's Angel. Have the dogs gone?'

'Yes, they've gone.'

'Then you must listen to me. We was diggin' and the ground gave way beneath us. We fell down 'ere into a God-forsaken vault of rotting corpses. A mighty stone slab fell on top and we can't get out. Horace has hurt his shoulder. We've got a lamp in here but no spade. I've made this 'ole with me 'ands but it'll take me all night to dig us out. Get a spade, Angel. Then you must open up this 'ole. You was a good boy before by throwin' up the stone on the roof and warnin' us. If you can do this for us, I'll pay you handsome.'

'I've got the spade here,' I said. 'I'll do what I can.'

I hesitated – wondering if I should run away. These were wicked men, I was sure, and I had no cause to help them in their ghoulish escapades. But I knew Jack Cutpurse and his nephew meant me no harm and were providing me with shelter and food. Where else could I go? The streets of town were already infested with boys like me, more often than not starving, diseased or injured in the gutter. I couldn't bear to return to Master Groundling or the workhouse again. So, once again, I had little choice. Wretched though this night had been, I couldn't leave two men to perish in a pit or to be found by the watchmen and strung up at the gallows for all to see.

Slowly I picked up the spade and dug into the earth. I couldn't help thinking of the change in circumstances. A few nights before, these rogues were digging me from my grave and here I was doing the same for them. But never again did I want to return to this gruesome place. Once more the moonlight crept across the ground in swirling puddles of silver as I looked down into the blinking eyes beneath the widening hole at my feet.

'You're doing most well, young Angel,' Jack Cutpurse called up to me. 'Just don't let that stone fall in here or we're done for. Throw me down the other spade and I'll dig from this side.'

I did as he asked and before long the hole was big enough for Jack to scramble through. As he emerged into the pale moonlight, he staggered towards me and raised his arm. I flinched, thinking he was about to strike me but instead he grabbed my hand and shook it vigorously. 'I'll never forget what you've done tonight, Angel. I wouldn't have blamed you for turnin' and runnin'. There's something about you that ain't normal. There's a lot of good in you. Where d'yer get it from?'

'I couldn't really leave you here, could I?' I smiled. 'After all, what would Tooth say if I'd left you here? And what about Mrs Dalrymple?'

'I think she'll have enough to say as it is. Come on, you must help me lift 'em both out of that hell hole.'

'Both?'

'Yeah, of course. We haven't gone through all this business to leave the corpse down there. Among all the filth and bones, there's a woman what's quite fresh. Just right for the doctor.'

'So that's what you do,' I said as it dawned on me. 'You come out to rescue sick people who have been buried by mistake and take them to a doctor to make them well again. After all, you found me in time. You're not villains after all.'

He looked at me and sighed. 'What it is to be an innocent child. I so wish it was true what you say. How do you mean we found you in time?'

'They buried me because they must have thought

I was dead. I now remember falling from a high window and after that I remember nothing. I must have been knocked senseless.'

'So you're not an angel at all?'

'I don't know what I am any more,' I said.

'I think you must be sent from on high. That strange picture of a face on your wrist shows you're no ordinary boy.'

'Yes, she's My Lady.' I smiled proudly. 'My friend for life.'

We returned to the hole to pull through Horace Dalrymple, who swore in rasps of steamy breath at the pain we caused him. While he lay writhing and groaning on the grass, Jack and I had to return to the hole to pull up the sack with its macabre contents. It was a struggle to load it as well as Horace into the wheelbarrow and push them towards the gates. By the time we'd all managed to climb over, pulling everything with us, the moon was sinking behind the church, the clouds were brightening and birds had begun singing. We trudged our way over cobbles, down alleys and through narrow streets, as dogs howled not far behind us. We all knew the watchmen and their eager hounds had returned to scour the graveyard – with daylight about to reveal its secrets.

I looked up at Jack and he looked at me. It seemed a miracle had saved us from perishing back there. Nothing was said but we both knew something or someone must have been watching over us. But neither of us was prepared to say who we thought it might be.

The mysterious doctor

----- Chapter 9 -----

'I hope yer don't mind me asking,' Tooth said as he sat cross-legged by the stove, puffing on a clay pipe, 'But why is it, seein' as you're a workhouse boy and no more than a chimney sweep, that you're such a gent?'

'How do you mean?' I asked wearily, keen to sleep off the night's horrors.

'The way yer speak. The way you are. Why ain't yer tongue as filthy as a sewer-rat? Yer talk like you've got a bit of breeding. Who learned yer them gentle manners?'

'They beat us at the workhouse if we didn't say "sir" or "madam" to the grown-ups in charge.'

'Nah, it's more than that. There's somethin' about yer, Angel. Somethin' special. I like yer.'

He offered me a puff on his pipe, which immediately set me coughing and spluttering. My throat had already been so blackened by smoke that my eyes were streaming in seconds. Tooth grinned while I wiped my face with my sleeve, as Turnip opened one eye to glare disapprovingly.

'How good are you at thievin'?' Tooth looked me up and down with a wink. 'Them fingers of yours used to lifting nice things?'

'No,' I said sharply. 'I don't think it's right to steal. Some of the children at the workhouse grabbed anything they could but they always caused terrible fights, got hurt or punished.'

'But the art, my friend,' he winked again and tapped his nose, 'is in not gettin' caught.'

'Maybe,' I said, copying his gesture and making him giggle. 'Or the art to not getting caught is not getting tempted!'

'That's as maybe, my friend. But needs must. It's

a matter of survival round 'ere.'

He continued to eye me up and down, clearly uncertain what to make of me, before tapping out his pipe on the stove and springing to his feet.

'I think it's time for breakfast,' he said, digging his fingers into a block of lard and dropping a dollop into the frying pan. He wiped his fingers down his torn breeches, whistled and winked.

'Looks like company,' he said, pointing to a face appearing at the top of the ladder – a girl's face, freckled and topped with a mop of ginger curls. She was chewing a length of bacon rind.

'I woke up with a corpse in the room,' she said, licking her fingers. 'D'yer want to come and look? Bulging eyes like glass marbles. Enough to turn me stomach, until I sniffed some bacon sizzlin'. Mam says there's a bit of fried bread for them that wants it.' Lotty Dalrymple took one look at the kittens snuggled on the sack and cackled like a witch. 'Mam'll soon drown that lot. So would Pa if he weren't hollerin' with pain. His bones must be broke, Mam says. She ain't happy, I can tell yer.'

'I don't know about breakfast,' I said. 'I'm ready for bed – we haven't been back from the churchyard very long and it was all very tiring.'

'I bet you didn't dare look at the corpse, Workhouse Boy,' Lotty sneered. 'You'd be too scared. Anyway, Mam says you'll have to help take it to the doctor, seein' how Pa can't push the barrow. He'll have to see the doctor himself to get his bones set. He says it hurts like damnation. He's swigged enough gin to stun a carthorse.'

'It's a bit late to take the dead body to the doctor,' I said in all innocence. 'It'll never recover.'

Lotty and Tooth shrieked.

'Don't you know nothin'?' Lotty cackled like a henhouse with a fox at its door. 'The doctor buys dead 'uns to cut up and find out about guts, you turnip head. Pa says this one'll fetch a guinea or more on account of her looking in good health.'

'Healthy but dead!' Tooth chuckled as he sizzled a pair of sausages in the pan.

'My Mam says if yer supposed to be an angel, why don't yer lay a healin' 'and on me Pa's bones?'

Before I could convince them that I was far from an angel, Jack Cutpurse climbed up the ladder and looked directly at me with his startled, ferrety eyes. 'Angel, my dear, I'd like a little chatter. We've been talking downstairs and I need a word.'

He moved towards me on his thin bandy legs

as Lotty disappeared back down the ladder, with another jarring cackle.

'You remain something of a mystery to us, Angel. Though you've told us your story, there's something about yer that troubles me. You see, if I takes yer out with me into the streets in broad daylight, what's to stop yer runnin' to the Bow Street Runners and tellin' tales, thereby sendin' us behind bars or to swing from the hangman's rope?'

'Why would I want to do that?' I was upset that he thought I'd do such a thing.

'It's just that you are privy to certain information about us that could be regarded in certain circumstances as being against the law…'

'Like digging up the dead?'

'Shsh, keep yer voice down. Someone might be listening.'

Tooth squealed with laughter as he prodded at the spitting sausages in the pan.

Without the glimmer of a smile, Jack Cutpurse looked over his shoulder as if the arm of the law was reaching out to grab him right there. 'What I'm trying to say, Angel, is that I need your word as a gent that you'll never bite the hand what's feedin' yer. In other words, you must promise me yer'll never breathe a word to no one about what yer hear or see here. Understand? I mean, with your himpeccable honesty, you may be tempted to speak out.'

'Of course I wouldn't get you into trouble,' I said. 'Why should I?'

'It's just that her downstairs don't think yer can be trusted. But Horace now thinks yer a good little fellow what's 'elped us. You got us back in one piece and with the stiff hintact. And I 'appen to think you could be of much use to us, particularly on account of your climbin' expertise. And I am sure we can be of benefit to you an' all – ain't that so, Tooth?'

'I'd say so, Uncle Jack. Anyone for a sausage?'

'So, young Angel, just try to think of what we do in the graveyard as helping them doctors learn their business. Yeah, we are just helping to make the world a better place by getting nice bodies for medics to work on – to rid our world of disease and the like.'

'Like smallpox?' I asked, as a vision of Mrs Brimstone flashed before me.

'Exactly. Now, the corpse downstairs is beginning to stink so we must get it to the doctor tonight as soon as it's dark and as soon as we've had some shut-eye. I'll need you to help me, seeing as Horace can hardly walk. He's going to see the doctor soon and will tell him to be ready after dark to receive us round the back of the hospital. I'll need you to keep those eyes of yours open and to carry my long stick in case of trouble, while I push the cart through town. Your reward will be a fine supper, a change out of those filthy clothes and I'll take yer to some entertainment for a real treat. How's that, my friend?'

'If that is what you want me to do, Mr Cutpurse, I shall do as I am asked.'

'Splendid. Now, eat up yer sausage and get to bed.'

It was a drab, blustery evening when we left the backyard through a rickety gate and entered an alley that stretched the length of a row of higgledy-piggledy back-to-back houses. The wind blew rain in eye-stinging squalls from a dark, churning sky. Mud and puddles underfoot were fed by dribbles and frequent torrents from overflowing gutters or broken drainpipes. Jack cursed as he pushed the barrow with its grisly load wrapped inside a now soaking sack, while I had to walk a few steps ahead, following his commands to turn left or right into other alleys or down gloomy passageways. I marched on, dodging the puddles and wielding the walking stick I'd been instructed to hold, with its heavy carved handle (that I'd been reliably informed had been used to crush many a rat's skull).

When we reached the streets, oil lamps had already been lit and their fizzing lights shone in yellow puddles across the shiny cobbles. The taverns and public-houses, with rush-lights burning inside, wafted their chimney smoke through the alleys. Even so, there appeared to be nobody stirring in this part of town; the windows of the houses were all closely shut and the streets through which we passed were noiseless and empty, apart from an occasional horse and cart clattering through the growing darkness. The only other sound was the squeaking wheel of the barrow and Jack's grunts whenever the cobbles became so bumpy that his arms shuddered, together with the body inside the sack. Once or twice he had to stop to poke a flopping arm back inside, as he glanced shiftily over his shoulder with a nonchalant whistle. Despite a few glances from passers-by, our progress through town was largely ignored by others, who were far more concerned with sheltering from the rain or dodging the slushy dollops of horse-muck strewn across the stinking puddles.

It was when we entered a narrow alley between two high walls that I realised why I was needed, or more precisely, the stick. A gang of unruly boys, not much older than me, were sprawled under a makeshift shelter of planks and crates. They called to us and jeered as we tried to squeeze past, one of them staggering out to demand to look in the sack. Despite Jack's shouts and curses, the boy wouldn't let him pass.

'I could do with a sack of grub,' the boy shouted, pulling back the sack and being stared back at by bulging eyes. Before the boy had time to squeal, Jack had snatched the stick from me and swished it back and forth, as if swatting flies. The boy squealed as Jack barged past with the barrow and on we strode, around a corner between begrimed buildings that poured swirling smoke from their chimneys.

'Just up here there's a passage what's at the back of the hospital,' Jack called, his head down against another downpour. From the passage, we descended steps into a yard piled with baskets brimming with foul-smelling rubbish, bloody bandages and festering bundles. Rats scurried through filthy puddles as we climbed the steps to a door. I lifted the latch with the stick as Jack dragged the sack up the steps behind me and into a dark room piled high with crates.

'Knock on that door there,' he told me, as he struggled to find a space for his gruesome delivery. I raised the stick and tapped three times on the door and stood to one side. The door slowly opened and a shadowy face emerged. 'What do you want?'

I tried to speak but couldn't. Jack darted over, stood in front of me and announced proudly, as if he had brought the finest equipment that money could buy, 'Your special delivery, doctor.'

'Ah, it's you. Bring it through. I want to see it before I pay.'

Jack pulled the sack up to the door. 'In you go, Angel.'

I shuffled into a dark corridor, with its sickly mixture of vile smells.

'Put it on the table in that room,' the doctor barked. Dark though it was, I could see his squat nose and wire spectacles. His voice sent a shiver through my bones. 'Hurry up.'

He brushed past me to shut the door, checking that no prying eyes could witness his barbaric trade. Jack puffed and panted to lift the sack. 'Very well, Doctor Brimstone. Give a hand, Angel.'

But I didn't. I ran from the room and hurtled down a maze of corridors. I had to get away from that terrible man. Even though I'd have enjoyed watching his horrified face when he saw I'd come back to life, I dreaded this cruel doctor ever seeing me again. I had no clue where I was running but I knew I had to get away from the shouts behind me. Still clutching the stick, I ran into a room, only to be confronted by the most horrific of sights.

On a table in the middle of the room, beneath an oil lamp strung above it, a man lay screaming while others held him down. At first I thought he was being robbed by a gang until I saw a large man in a bloodied apron step forward, carrying a saw and a knife. He was a surgeon about to operate on the thrashing patient. He calmly pushed a rag into the patient's mouth to stifle the screams, while one of the helpers sat on the man's chest. The surgeon raised the knife and held it just above the patient's knee, which glistened raw and horribly black under the lamp. 'Hold still, man,' the surgeon shouted.

101

'This will be over in one minute and the offending limb removed.' He grasped the patient's thigh with one hand and, gripping the long knife in his other, he sliced it across the leg. I looked away in horror, unable to believe what was happening. At the chilling sound of steel sawing through bone, I looked up again, squinting through my fingers, to see the last strokes of the saw. As if in triumph, the surgeon shouted, 'There, gentlemen! Within one minute the femoral artery will be tied with two stout ligatures, a strip of lint placed between the flaps and the stump raised.'

I turned and ran, my hand over my mouth, and scuttled down more corridors. Next, I came to a long room lined with beds along opposite walls. Each bed was occupied, in some cases by two or three people. A large table was cluttered with pots, pans and flickering candles. A cat rubbed round my ankles before springing after a mouse scampering under the beds. It was only as I looked up that I realised the man sitting on the nearest bed with his arm in a sling looked familiar.

'Fancy seein' you, Angel,' he said. 'You've come to take me back, I hope. Got the barrow?'

'Yes, Mr Dalrymple,' I said. 'Are you feeling better?'

'Far from it. But I'm not staying here. Broken shoulder and ribs. They've bled me and given me some foul mixture and charged me a fortune for the pleasure. Ain't that so, Doctor Taggi?'

I turned to see a tall lean man with dark skin, long black hair and the darkest eyes I had ever seen. He was dressed very elegantly and was like no one I had ever seen before. His unusual boots had leather pouches at the calves and ribbons tied round his moleskin breeches just below the knee. I must have stared, open-mouthed, for he smiled before speaking directly to me. His voice, with its rich, unfamiliar accent mesmerised me. 'I am afraid, young man, that some doctors do charge highly. If I had my way, it would not be so. Have you come for your father?'

'He's no son of mine,' Horace grunted.

'Maybe not,' the man smiled, showing the whitest of teeth. Most adults I knew had either brown teeth or none at all. 'I can now see,' he went on, 'that there is no family likeness.'

The doctor suddenly stopped speaking and stared at me. His dark eyes narrowed and there was a long awkward silence. He stepped towards me and stretched out his hand and clasped mine. I was frightened by his startled expression. He looked down and whispered, 'Sitala.'

I was so scared, I snatched my hand away and ran. He called after me but I was now in such mad panic that I raced down the corridor, desperate to get out of the building. Darting round a corner, I ran straight into a man striding towards me. It was Jack.

'This is an abominable place, Angel. I want to get away, too. But we've done well.' He smiled and held up a gold coin. 'We've got good money for our efforts. We'll take Horace home and we'll all eat well tonight.'

Ragamuffins and rapscallions

—— *Chapter 10* ——

I was woken by the spattering of sausages. At first I thought it was rain beating against the glass, as I emerged from a disturbing dream. A dream about bulging-eyed bodies in sacks, severed limbs and a tall, mystical Indian doctor chasing after me down never-ending tunnels.

'Mornin', Angel.' Tooth, as usual, stood at the stove with the frying pan. 'You are in for a treat today, my friend. It's market day, hence the early start.

Rich pickin's and fun to be had by all. Uncle Jack will be takin' you and me to see a few sights, I can tell yer. Ever been to market day before?'

'No,' I said. 'I don't think I have.'

'Yer'd certainly know it if yer had, Angel. The street is crammed with riches.'

As dawn was breaking, pink clouds bubbled up above the jagged rooftops where a smoky mist lingered. Uncle Jack, armed with his trusty stick, led the way into town with keen loping strides. Tooth, being much shorter than me, had to run to keep up but that didn't stop him chatting excitedly all the way as we dodged the puddles and other walkers through the busy alleys. Straggling groups of labourers were already on their way to work and the nearer we got to market, the greater number of traders we passed: men and women with fish-baskets on their heads, barrow boys with apples and flagons of cider, milk-women with pails; donkey-carts laden with vegetables or piled with pig carcasses. As soon as we turned into a street packed with market stalls, I stood still, open-mouthed. The noise, bustle and smells rolled over us like the smoke belching down from the chimney-tops. The ground was covered, nearly ankle-deep, with filth and mire, and a thick steam rose from the reeking bodies of cattle, mingling with the smoky fog. Tied up to posts by the gutter were lines of cows and horses where farmhands, butchers, drovers, hawkers, errand boys and beggars shouted above the noise. I could hardly hear Tooth's chattering above the barking of dogs, the bellowing of cattle, the squawking of fowl, the bleating of sheep and goats, the grunting and squeaking of pigs, the ringing of bells, the cries of hawkers, the shouts, oaths, and quarrelling on all sides; the bawling and bickering, whistling and wailing, cackling and caterwauling. Ragged children and grubby vagabonds, some already drunk and spilling from the ale houses, ran, staggered or merely slumped between the brimming stalls.

'For you, my boy,' Uncle Jack pressed half a warm bun into my hand. Tooth was already eating the other half (more like sucking it, without his teeth). I saw a bread roll poking from Jack's pocket, and yet I hadn't noticed his cunning sleight of hand as we passed the baker's cart. Nor did I see how Tooth acquired a twist of liquorice and a silk cravat.

I watched the buying and selling of animals and while I observed the traders bartering their wares, being shoved one way then jostled another, I was unaware of Tooth's antics entirely. Eventually we met up by an auctioneer's pen, stinking of manure and wet snorting horses, where I was amazed to see Tooth's bulging shirt, pockets and sleeves.

'Just a few things for later,' he grinned.

'A fine collection indeed,' Uncle Jack winked. His jacket, too, seemed well-stuffed.

'Leather?' he asked Tooth.

'Would I let you down, Uncle Jack? A couple of wallets.'

Judging by the regular scuffles and yells around us, it was clear there were many other thieves at work. It made me feel uncomfortable and I was keen to move on.

'And move on we shall, my dear,' Uncle Jack whispered. 'I shall show yer what 'appens to them nasty pickpockets what are so bad… that they get caught red-handed. Follow me, boys…'

With stick aloft, Jack led the way down a passage and over a wooden footbridge. We all held our noses, for the putrid stench rising from below was unbearable. Among the bubbling sewage, I saw a dead horse half-submerged in the open sewer. We continued our way between half-timbered dwellings, often with damp washing strung across the street and half-naked children running among scrawny hens and sluggish rats. Eventually we came to an open square where a few traders were setting up stalls and a crowd was gathering.

'It is wise never to get caught in the act of thieving or skulduggery,' Jack said, 'For you are about to see that pilfering from the rich may result in a heavy penalty. That's why one has to be careful, hey, Tooth?'

'Exactly so, uncle. Steal from a lord and you'll get transported for life. Take the same from a nobody and it's a mere dose of the pillory. There's nothin' like a public floggin' for a good day out, ain't that so, Uncle Jack?'

'To teach a lesson to them ragamuffins and rapscallions.'

'Yeah,' Tooth was now crying with giggles, 'Them muttonheads, guttersnipes and dirty ne'er-do-wells!'

I couldn't help chuckling, too, at their well-rehearsed performance, but I stopped as a hush descended over the crowd. Constables appeared in the middle of the square and between them they escorted a hunched figure, an elderly man in a ragged brown coat. The poor specimen looked thoroughly miserable, like a wild creature forced to perform in a circus. For a circus is what the scene became, with the crowd erupting into jeers and raucous name-calling, and pushing as one into a semi-circle around the wooden frame in which the man was being secured. He had to place both wrists and his neck into the appropriate slots before the hinged upper frame was lowered and locked into place. A crier called above the crowd that the man's hideous crime was begging within sight of the bishop's palace. The baying crowd seemed unconcerned as to the actual offence, being more intent on sport and in pelting the sobbing man with whatever they could find. People were selling bags of rotten eggs, mouldy potatoes, rancid butcher's offal and buckets of pigs' blood and dung for the crowd to throw. A gaggle of women from the fish market arrived with baskets of herring entrails. A chimney sweep sold paper bags filled with soot and ash. As soon at the constables moved away and blew a whistle, the frenzied hurling began. Jack and Tooth joined in the taunting, cheering every time a projectile hit its target. It disturbed me to see their delight in the humiliation of the poor victim, whose crime was surely nothing as compared to their own. His head and body were soon so smothered in foul-smelling filth that he was barely recognisable as a fellow human. Maybe if he'd been a brazen unrepentant murderer I might have felt differently, but it was unnerving to be the only one in the crowd to be upset by the whole spectacle. Once more I was unsure why I felt this way, that I just didn't belong here, and it disturbed me.

'Cheer up, Angel,' Jack said as he took a bite from one of the rolls he'd stolen, 'it's all good fun. What next, boys? We could visit my friend Gallimaufry Garderobe's freak show. He'll let us look at some of the things for free, I'm sure – like the girl who can juggle with snakes, a real Indian prince and a boy with three eyes and a beard. What d'yer think, Tooth?'

'Hangin',' he grinned. 'I want to see someone swing.'

'Very well. It ain't far and by my reckoning.' He looked up at the clock tower. 'The execution will be another hour or so. If we go now ahead of the rest, we'll get a good view.'

Once more Jack held up his stick and we followed, weaving through the milling crowds and on towards the gallows. With mouth full of bread, Tooth looked up at me with a wink, as his fingers lifted a spoon from a merchant's stall as we passed.

'To the gallows!' he spluttered.

'To the gallows!' Jack echoed.

I didn't say a word. Reluctantly I followed, unaware that the worst display of human nature and cruelty was yet to come.

To the gallows

he streets crackled with excitement and expectation. As we walked through towering spiked gates into the prison yard, a crowd was already gathering boisterously. I'd never seen so many hundreds of jostling people, let alone been in the midst of such an excited atmosphere. All types were here, including gentlemen in top hats and ladies in fine silks, as well as the usual waifs and urchins hoping for pickings. All attention was directed towards a wooden platform and scaffold, like an empty theatre-stage waiting for the grand performance to begin.

'See them gentry up there behind them windows?' Jack said, pointing to faces peering down at us through the glass above the platform. 'They eats their victuals and sips their wines in warmth and comfort with a grand view of the drop. It costs 'em a fair few guineas for the privilege, an' all. But as it's a fine day, we can see just as well for nothin'.'

Indeed, the day was now bright and fine, apart from a cold wind, but inside the prison yard, surrounded as we were by high walls topped with wire and spikes, we were sheltered and reasonably warm. I was just grateful it wasn't raining, but even a deluge would never deter this crowd.

'There's other good seats up close for a price, if yer want to hear the prisoner's last words as well as his cries, gurgles and final croak. But I reckon we'll see the lot here for free. Today's hanging will bring an even greater crowd. It's Crispin Ramshaw, a highway robber, killer and housebreaker. He'll be one to watch by all accounts, and I shouldn't wonder if they don't leave him hanging overnight. Let's hope so.'

Sellers mingled in the crowd with their souvenirs for sale: tiny model gallows, nooses and little twists of rope said to be from the previous hanging, although we all knew they couldn't all be. Printed accounts of the prisoner's crimes, copies of his confession and final speech were sold as pamphlets to those in the paid seats, as they were more likely to be able to read. People around us sat knitting, eating, singing, swigging ale or engaging in playful banter, which steadily increased as the tension mounted, especially when the tolling bell from a nearby church announced the cart with the prisoner was on its way.

'Let's 'ope he wriggles a lot,' Tooth grinned and his eyes lit up at the prospect. 'The last one I saw here took over 'alf an hour to croak. Nice.'

As soon as the horses pulling the prisoner's cart snorted at the gates, a deafening cheer rose from the crowd, with hats thrown, handkerchiefs waved and kisses blown by many of the catcalling women. When the prisoner himself came into view, everyone surged forward, which meant Tooth and I saw nothing. The cheering and applause changed to hurled insults and obscenities, as well as handfuls of sand grabbed from underfoot. The roars and

115

screams were now far more menacing and the angry taunts bounced back at us off the high walls in a wave of sheer hatred. By the time people around us moved so we could catch a glimpse, the cart had arrived at the platform and I first saw the object of all the abuse and outrage. He stood defiantly, a handsome figure impeccably dressed and clearly of great excitement to the women at the front.

One of the prison warders untied a rope which bound the prisoner to the cart. The skittish horses, clearly nervous at all the noise and mud-slinging, were coaxed by the horseman to reverse the cart up to the platform under the arm of the gallows. Another enormous cheer went up when, as if from nowhere, a cloaked masked figure appeared on the steps behind the platform. He was the hangman, dressed entirely in black; black hood, gloves and cloak buttoned down to his feet. He slowly ascended the steps and stood totally still with arms folded, the only movement being the stirring of his cloak in the breeze. Everyone watched the agonisingly slow edging of the cart into position under the noose. For the first time, the prisoner's bravado seemed to waver when he saw the daunting figure of the hangman. With his wrists tied behind his back, the prisoner was unable to gesture, but I felt certain he would have done so to both crowd and executioner if he were able. As it was, he shouted and protested, but the roar of the crowd soon drowned his taunts. He spat at one of the warders and the whole multitude went totally wild. Armies of constables ran to restrain the mob from storming the platform and it was only the raised hand of the otherwise motionless hangman that quelled the frenzy. The tension was almost unbearable.

'We're lucky to see this hangman,' Jack said, sounding very much the seasoned spectator. 'He's known as Titus the Rope. He don't do it so often these days and he's the only one what dresses like that, with the full hood and gown. No one knows what he really looks like or his proper name. Sometimes it's Titus Twist on account of the way he gives the noose a little turn before slippin' it over their heads. Just you watch.'

Crispin Ramshaw, in burgundy waistcoat, velvet breeches, black leather boots with silver spurs and a stunning crimson cravat inside the white lace of his shirt, was a sight to behold as he shouted insults at all of us. He cursed and hurled vile oaths at all and sundry. The responding hisses and shouts from all around reached fever pitch as the hangman stepped onto the cart. Holding the reluctant prisoner's elbow, he guided him backwards a few paces to stand immediately below the noose which he checked was at exactly the right height. From his cloak he took a blindfold and then reached out to remove Crispin Ramshaw's cravat from his neck. That was when all hell let loose. Though his ankles were tied, the prisoner tried to kick, then head-butt his executioner. The women at the front screeched and swooned, throwing some of their clothes onto the platform. Ramshaw turned and raised his arms high behind his back, somehow managing to claw at the hangman's throat with his tied hands. Titus the Rope, more concerned with his hood being raised, stepped backwards and in the ensuing scuffle I noticed something like a necklace slip from under his hood. By now the crowd was screaming like never before and all manner of objects were pelting the platform. Once more the hangman raised his hand for calm, but it was a long time coming.

Furious at having to remove his cravat and loudly refusing to wear the blindfold, the prisoner had to be restrained by constables so that Titus the Rope could lower the noose over his head. Just before he did so, he slowly, almost ceremoniously, twisted the rope – to the enthusiastic applause of the crowd.

'Told yer,' Jack winked. 'He likes the prisoner to spin a bit as he chokes!'

As he brought the noose down over the prisoner's head, the hangman rested it very gently on his throat, like an animal-tamer tethering a wild beast, as if hurting Crispin Ramshaw was the last thing he wanted to do. The crowd fell eerily silent as the hangman tightened the noose and stepped back from the cart onto the platform. Once more he folded his arms and remained perfectly still. The prisoner, now standing alone on the cart, also fell silent and stopped his ranting, kicking and shaking of his head. Instead, far more chillingly, he began to sob quietly, just like a small child. A breathless hush descended over the entire scene and no one stirred. Even the breeze seemed to die and the only sound was the distant tolling of the bell.

The hangman continued to wait, his head turned towards the horseman standing very still, holding the reins. A pigeon fluttered down to the scaffold, unaware of the drama and what was about to happen. The hangman raised his hand, pointing a steady finger at the horseman and holding the pose before dropping his arm. Immediately the horseman tugged at the horses and, with a rattle of their harness, a creak of the cart and a stamp of their hooves, the cartwheels jolted into motion. As it trundled forward, the cart spilled its load off the back and the crowd erupted once more. The prisoner fell, the rope tightened and the whole gallows shook, as did the ground beneath us, with everyone stamping as they cheered. That was when I looked away.

'Look at him thrashing,' Tooth shouted with glee.

I felt sick. It wasn't just the hideous sight of a dangling fellow human in his final desolate moments, but it was those bloodcurdling cries from the mob delighting in the whole barbaric spectacle. It troubled me, as I just didn't belong here, nor did I want to belong to the human race any more. I stared at the ground, desperate for this torture to end. While all eyes were fixed on the twisting body in its final death throes, my head remained bowed. I couldn't bear to see the man's contorted face and jerking limbs. Instead, I glanced sideways, across the platform where I saw the hangman moving quietly away from the scene. I watched him descend the steps, catching the hem of his cloak and stumbling slightly. It was in that instant, probably unseen by anyone else, that I saw something that surprised and amazed me. I had glimpsed the hangman's secret… and I was stunned.

'Sometimes someone will grab his legs and pull 'em to speed things up,' Jack said. 'But not this one. They'll keep him wrigglin' as long as they can to show any other highway robbers what to expect. They likes to teach us all a lesson.'

'What sort of lesson? That it's not a good idea to be a thief?' I asked. He gave me a sideways glance but he didn't smile.

'That's it,' Tooth shouted. 'He's gone. He's stopped twitchin'.'

The crowd whistled and clapped before gradually dispersing. First to leave were the gentry in their coaches, having been helped down from the flat roofs where they'd toasted the hangman with glasses of their finest port. The constables were holding people back from the gallows, from touching the body or from snipping souvenirs off his clothes. The hangman and prison warders had already left in a spray of sand from the cart in which they'd arrived. Jack's eyes were still fixed on the now motionless Crispin Ramshaw. 'I wonder,' he said, approaching a constable to ask, 'Is he to hang for long or will the doctors be havin' him to cut up?'

'Not this one,' the man answered with a wry smile. 'This is one for all to see for as long as possible. He'll stay here till tomorrow's executions, then be chained in an iron gibbet to hang at the very crossroads where he did his crimes, his eyes to be pecked out by crows. All highway robbers need to be warned by the fate of young Ramshaw here.'

We left the prison yard, shuffling out with everyone else through the iron gates. Jack looked down at me and placed his hand on my shoulder.

'We can come back tomorrow if you like.'

'No thank you.'

'Yeah!' Tooth was more enthusiastic than ever. 'Someone told me they're hangin' a girl what's fourteen what poisoned her father with arsenic in his rabbit stew.'

I must have stared at him with a look of utter revulsion. 'I don't want to see a hanged body ever again.'

Jack stopped walking, turned round and looked up at the black prison gates.

'But you will, my dear. That very same one. We're coming back to get him. At midnight.'

The hangman's secret

—— Chapter 12 ——

'Y ou'll do as you're told,' Mrs Dalrymple shrieked at me, her neck puffing up like a bullfrog's. 'You'll earn your keep like everyone else in this house. I'm all for kicking you out on the streets or sellin' yer corpse to the doctor but it's Jack what wants yer. He says Tooth and you'll be able to squeeze through them bars of the prison gate. If you dare try and run off, my Horace'll kill yer even with his arm strapped up. Upset him and yer'll have me to deal with.'

Horace dared to speak for himself. 'After our antics in the graveyard, this'll be child's play.'

My look of horror at returning to the hanged prisoner after dark obviously didn't impress them, so it was Lotty's turn to convince me next.

'Ever heard of the King's Evil?' she asked. 'The doctors call it scrofula.'

'No, I've never heard of it.'

'It's a disease what Mam's got. Makes her neck swell and feel sore. It's called King's Evil as they say the touch of a king's hand'll cure it.'

'The only trouble is, the king ain't one of our personal friends,' Horace added. 'So we need the next best thing to make her better.'

'What's that?' I asked, dreading the answer.

'A snip of the hangman's rope. It has special powers.' Lotty sounded like an expert. 'If you can get a bit of the rope tonight, we'll put it on Mam's neck and she'll get better. Will yer help?'

Horace brought his face right up to mine. 'And we'll be able to sell some of it, too. Everyone wants a bit of hangman's rope round here. It cures all sorts but it's also very lucky.'

124

'It wasn't very lucky for the prisoner,' I said.

'Don't try to be clever,' he snapped. 'People pay good money for real hanging rope. It brings a lot of luck at card games and gamblin'. Your job is to get through that gate, being the skinniest of us, and clamber up the scaffold with a knife between yer teeth and just cut down the rope. Nothin' to it. Easy.'

'What about the body on the end of it?' I asked, not daring to imagine the answer.

'It'll fall down, that's all. True, we'd like to get him for the doctor but we'll never get him over or through the gate. If Tooth can also squeeze through the bars, he'll be with yer to look after the corpse. You won't have to touch it.'

'But what if someone sees us?' I had to ask … the most obvious of my fears.

'They won't. Too dark and they never guard the yard on account that no one can get in. They don't reckon on little urchins like you being able to squeeze through the gate bars. After all, who's ever heard of someone wanting to break into gaol? Jack and me'll be waiting for yer at the gate so yer'll come to no harm.'

I knew I had no choice. If I didn't do the dreadful deed, I'd be instantly punished, homeless or worse.

There was nothing I could do but eat the supper provided, go to bed early as instructed and brace myself for being woken before midnight – when once again we'd be prowling the misty darkness in the company of the dead.

The final clang of midnight drifted over the moonlit rooftops. The bell tower once more fell silent, as did the smoky back-streets and alleys… until footsteps creaked on the wooden footbridge, with the sinister squeak of a barrow's wheel.

'You should have greased that wheel with pig fat,' Horace grunted.

'I don't see why we had to bring it tonight.' Jack protested, 'Yer said yerself we'll not get the corpse through the gate.'

'Not all of him.'

I stopped in my tracks. Whatever did Horace mean by that?

'Cor it stinks here worse than before,' Tooth said, pinching his nose.

'If either of you misbehave tonight, that sewer

down there is where you'll end up,' Horace growled. 'But do your job well and there'll be wages for all.' I wasn't so sure I wanted such wages, as I gingerly followed the three of them over the bridge and towards the dreaded prison gates.

It wasn't as easy as they'd thought to get me through the bars. At one point, I thought I was stuck and it took a lot of pushing to get me through. Tooth managed to wriggle under the gate after using a shovel from the barrow to dig out the earth beneath. Once we were inside the yard, it felt unnervingly quiet after all the noise of the crowd earlier. Jack lit a lantern and passed it through to me.

'Keep it covered with this sack as much as you can. Only use it when you must.'

Next he passed me a long sharp knife and another to Tooth, who was already chattering excitedly despite Horace's repeated warnings to 'shut yer mouth, Cutpurse.'

As we both skulked off into total darkness, our whispers were edged with fear. 'Can you see the platform?' Tooth kept asking. He used Jack's stick, rather like a blind man's, by poking it in front of us to tap against any obstacles.

'Not yet. I can't see anything.' Behind us I could see a faint glow from a street lantern back at the gates, where Jack and Horace waited, trying not to look suspicious – even though they couldn't look anything but. A new moon sliced the blackness above, brushing the wall spikes with specs of silver.

'Shsh. Can yer 'ear it?' Tooth stood still and we listened to a steady creaking just ahead of us. We both knew it was the gallows where the body was slowly swaying to and fro in the breeze. We crept towards it and stopped when the stick tapped the edge of the platform. It was hard to imagine this was where thousands of pairs of eyes had been fixed a few hours before. I only hoped that no eye was able to see what was about to happen.

'I've just had a thought,' Tooth croaked. 'What if he's not dead yet?'

The thought had already crossed my mind, too. 'But you said he was dead this afternoon. He couldn't last this long... could he?' I didn't sound very convinced.

'It has been known,' Tooth was now sounding worryingly uncertain, 'for them to be cut down only to leap up again.'

'Are you sure?' I took out the knife just to give me courage.

'Take the sack off the lantern so we can see him.'

I did as he said but I wished I hadn't. The light flickered up into the gallows where the body swung directly above us. The man's face stared down at me, the tongue lolling from the mouth and the open eyes fixed on mine. I looked away and scuttled to the back of the platform. It was as I was crawling through the sand that my fingers touched something cold. I shone the lantern and in the pool of light I saw a fine silver chain with a gold circle attached to it, like a coin. But it wasn't a coin, it was a pendant with a face engraved on it. I snatched it from the ground and squinted at it in total amazement. It was the very same face as 'My Lady' on my wrist. How could she be here on a necklace? I was sure it must have been the one I'd seen fall from the hangman.

'Hurry up,' Tooth called. 'Climb up there and cut him down. Make sure we get as much rope as you can.'

As I climbed up the scaffold with the knife in my mouth, the lantern casting its ghoulish shadows below, I felt my palms sweating and heart thumping. I clambered out on the long arm of the gallows, knowing only too well that it was a long drop. Just under me was the swinging body of Crispin Ramshaw. His head was flopped to one side. I stretched out my arm, reached down with the knife clenched in my fist and sliced at the rope. Strands snapped and, with the weight it was carrying, the rope stretched and suddenly broke. The body fell with a thud, groaning with a bloodcurdling gurgle, and sending Tooth scurrying under the platform with a whimper.

By the time I'd climbed back down, I was ready to run. I wasn't going near the body. 'Are you coming?' I called.

'Here I am,' Tooth emerged from the shadows holding a sack in one hand and what looked like a small meat clever in the other.

'Did you cut a good length of rope?' I asked.

'Yeah. And the rest.'

'The rest?'

'Both his hands.'

I stared at him in shocked disbelief and shuddered. 'That's terrible. Whatever for?'

'Uncle Jack told me to. It's a well-known fact that the hands of a hanged man have amazin' powers.

130

Come on. You can blow out that lantern now and we'll head for the gates.'

Once more we headed through the deepest darkness. Before we reached the gates, Tooth grabbed my arm and whispered. 'Shsh, don't move.'

We froze at the sound of raised voices nearby. Even more chilling was the all-too-familiar snarling of ferocious dogs. Neither of us dared move. We heard a man demanding an answer. 'What are you doing with that barrow here at this time of night?'

'I'm afraid, constable,' I heard Jack saying, 'that my friend here with his bad arm has had too much gin and I'm about to carry him home.'

'I saw you here earlier at the hanging, didn't I?'

'That's right, constable. I spoke to you. You all did an excellent job with such a crowd. I so admired your h'expertise.'

I'd never heard Jack sound so charming. By now the dogs were barking madly and growling through the bars of the gate. Their handler shouted above their noise. 'Those dogs can smell something in there. I think there's someone inside the prison yard. We'll soon see when I let them loose inside.'

Jack sounded worried now. 'Really, constable? Will those big dogs get through the bars?'

Tooth and I still hadn't moved and the noise of the dogs and their chains rattling against the gates was terrifying. If they got through, we'd be torn apart. The yelps and howls chilled me to the bone. The constable spoke again. 'Listen, I'm sure there's someone in there but the hounds can't get between the bars. It'll only take me a minute to get the key to these gates. Stand there and keep watch while I fetch the key. You seem like a trustworthy soul.'

'Of course, sir. I'd be very pleased to help.'

As soon as the dogs had gone, we heard Jack whistle to us, with Horace cursing in the background. We rushed to the gate, passed the sack through and then tried to squeeze between the bars ourselves. They were dripping with dogs' saliva. Tooth, with more digging, wriggled underneath but I became wedged at the hip. I just couldn't get myself through and when Jack pulled me, I screamed with pain. I stretched on the ground with my head and shoulders outside the gates, my hips being chewed by the bars and my legs inside the yard.

'Quick, move yerself, boy,' Horace shouted. With his spare hand he grabbed my hair and pulled.

It was then we heard the choking of dogs pulling on their chains, on their way back. The bars gnawed my flesh and I felt blood on my scraped skin. 'Twist round. Roll over!' Tooth squealed at me. I tried to turn and free myself from the iron grip of the bars, with the three of them tugging and twisting me.

'Go,' Horace hissed. 'We'll get away and let him take his chance. Leave him to the dogs.'

'No,' Tooth cried. 'We can't do that.'

'Turn more on your side,' Jack was dragging me over onto my side. 'That's it, yer movin'.'

At last I slithered through the bars and slumped on the ground outside the gate. Before I knew it, I'd been lifted up, dumped in the barrow and whisked away. We were rumbling over cobbles in the dark as we heard the gates clanging open and the dogs howling once more.

'Consider yerself lucky,' Horace snarled.

'It must be the hangman's rope,' Jack said. 'I told yer it was lucky.'

Tooth added breathlessly, 'Not as lucky as his hands. I got both of 'em!'

'Perfect,' Jack whistled cheerily as he put down the barrow for me to get out, to hobble with sore and bleeding hips.

'Good boys. Well done. An excellent night's work.'

I wasn't so sure, as once more we headed for

home through misty streets, eerily silent beneath a hazy moon that glimpsed our despicable deeds before hiding in shame behind the clouds.

'Put a bit of that on yer neck, woman,' Horace called as he dropped the noose on the floor. 'Or if yer'd rather...' He lifted up a severed hand and slammed it on the table. 'Here's something to bring more than a cure. This is magic itself.'

He picked up the other hand with a smile. 'An extra bit of luck. It's got a gold ring on the finger. I think we all deserve a dram and sausages before bed.'

It was well after three o'clock in the morning before I curled up on the mattress in the attic. The others continued talking, smoking and drinking long after I fell asleep. But after the torment of the last few hours, I couldn't sleep for long. I was troubled by so many of the disturbing things I'd seen and heard – but there was even worse to come. Without moving, I lay listening to the hushed conversation nearby, above the sizzling of the frying pan.

'All you have to do is melt the candle like this...' I opened an eye to see Horace standing at the stove as if demonstrating some new recipe. 'And then… pass me the dead hand… just dip the fingers in the wax…'

'What happens next?' Tooth asked with wide eyes.

'The wax hardens. And we've now made our own hand of glory.'

'For hundreds of years, the art of housebreaking has been blessed with a special secret…'

It was Jack's voice next, soft and secretive as if he were casting a magic spell. 'The hand of glory has long been used by robbers in the dead of night to protect them from dangers. You see, the hand of a hanged murderer is a much prized possession and has been a part of witchcraft since the beginning of time itself. If a housebreaker takes it with him into the house to be robbed just after midnight, it will work its magic as soon as he lights one of the fingers and leaves the hand to burn, spreading its mysterious powers all through the house. Wisps of smoke drift their hypnotic fumes. Anyone in the building, savage dogs included, will sleep without stirring for as long as the hand burns – apart from the burglar himself. He can go around the house and make as much noise as he chooses but so long as the hand of glory is alight, the sleeping magic lets

135

him take whatever he wishes and disappear without trace.'

He puffed on his pipe as Tooth sat absorbed by the magic of his uncle's spellbinding whisper.

'And we'll be using it tomorrow night,' Horace announced coldly, breaking the spell with a sinister chuckle. 'We're taking you and Angel to rob the bishop's palace stuffed with treasures worth a fortune.'

'I don't think Angel will like that,' Tooth said.

'He'll have no choice,' Horace answered abruptly. 'He nearly got us all caught tonight so it's about time he learnt this business properly. We'll make a housebreaker out of him yet.'

I lay very still, even though I wanted to run and hide. If my mind hadn't yet been made up, Horace's next idea convinced me I had to act soon. Their plans were turning more terrifying by the minute and I grew more scared and horrified.

'With my bad shoulder, I can't work in the day and I can't dig the graveyards at night, either. There's no money coming in so I've got the answer. The doctor still wants bodies, eh?'

'True.'

'He wants 'em the fresher the better. True?'

'True.'

'But diggin' 'em up is hard work and a risk, true?'

'True.'

'So why don't we kill our own?'

'What?!'

'There are plenty of beggars and vagabonds about that no one will miss. We just get the boys here to approach one in the street to lead down a dark alley, saying there's a bowl of hot broth on offer… and we're waitin' with a rope. Simple. Bodies freshly strangled then delivered to the doctor, still warm. No questions. We'll earn many guineas a night. Easy.'

There was a long pause as they sucked on their pipes.

'Sounds good to me,' Jack said with a cough.

'What do you think, Tooth?'

'Worth a try.'

'So that's the next few nights planned.' Horace cleared his throat and spat into the fire.

'I might bring Lotty with us. She'll be able to lure a few of the women into our trap. It's about time my daughter learnt how to earn a few shillings for herself.'

I couldn't believe what I was hearing. Surely

they'd never do such things. But by the way they continued their vile plotting, I knew I could stay there no longer. A clear voice inside my head was telling me this was wicked and I should go. It told me I must do far better than this.

I had to plan when to get away. If they caught me trying to escape, I'd be at great risk. And, of course, I had nowhere to go. But I reasoned once more that when you've got nothing in the world, you've got nothing in the world to lose. However, I remembered that I did have something now. Something that delighted yet puzzled me. I reached into my pocket where I felt the chain and pendant I'd found under the gallows. I thought of the hangman and his secret. I thought of my own unanswered questions that wouldn't go away. Questions that kept me awake. Questions about myself.

I lay still for a long time, listening to the heavy breathing of others now sound asleep. As the grey light of dawn turned to a pinkish smudge at the attic window, I knew it was time to get up and creep away forever. The house was silent apart from the snores and snuffles of its heavy sleepers. The only eyes to open as I crept down the ladder were Turnip's, but she just stretched, curled into a tighter ball and returned to her slumbers.

I climbed out through a small window beside a snoring Mrs Dalrymple, with the severed hand clutched around her neck. How glad I was to leave this gruesome house for the cool stillness of a new day outside… a new life. But I had no doubt life could be snatched from me at any moment if my escape should be discovered. I had to get away fast to who knew where? After all, I'd never known freedom before. A new journey was about to start, I thought to myself as I landed with a thud in the street. A journey to find the truth. A journey to discover the mystery of the hangman.

THE CURSE OF THE SPECKLED MONSTER

BOOK TWO

TWIST OF THE HANGMAN

JOHN TOWNSEND

The Twist of the Hangman

ike a lost soul, I wandered aimlessly through the empty, grey streets of the city. Soon I came to where the market had been a bustling rumpus the day before. Now the street was strewn with filth and debris, like the aftermath of a battle. Mud and dung squelched underfoot and the air was thick with vile odours. Heaps of ragged children sprawled in doorways and across the steps of public houses, like the slain. They crawled between battered boxes and crates, some sleeping inside them or huddled under stinking sacks. Most of these poor

143

specimens looked dazed, diseased or deformed and I knew only too well this was where I would end up if I didn't find a way to survive. I vowed never to end up like these hopeless souls. These streets were just too dangerous, especially as I now risked being kidnapped or worse by those from whom I'd just escaped.

I was soon to discover that other dangers, as well as unimagined secrets yet unrevealed, would crash into my world and change me beyond my wildest dreams.

Discover how

THE CURSE OF THE SPECKLED MONSTER

(*smallpox*) *was finally slain in* **BOOK TWO**

Key dates behind Cephas Catchpole's story and beyond...

1787   The first prisoners were transported from Britain to Australia.

1788   William Brodie was hanged at the Tolbooth in Edinburgh. A city councillor by day, Brodie was a housebreaker by night. A crowd of 40,000 watched his execution.

1789   Catherine Murphy, a counterfeiter, became the last woman in Britain to be sentenced to death by burning (although she was actually strangled before being burned at the stake).

1790   Joseph Guillotine proposed a new method of execution in France: a machine designed to cut off the condemned person's head as painlessly as possible. Burning at the stake for women convicted of treason was abolished in Britain and replaced by drawing to the place of execution and hanging.

1791   William Wilberforce again introduced a motion in the British Parliament for the abolition of the slave trade but lost by a vote of 163 to 88.

1792   James Penny, a Liverpool slave trader, was presented with a magnificent silver vase for speaking in favour of the slave trade to a parliamentary committee. Liverpool's Penny Lane was named after him.

1793   France declared war on Britain and the Netherlands. In this year of the French Revolution, Marie Antoinette was beheaded. War continued until the final defeat of Napoleon at the Battle of Waterloo in 1815.

1794   Horatio Nelson lost his right eye during a military operation in Corsica.

1795   Mungo Park, a Scottish surgeon, sailed from England on behalf of the British African Association to search for the Niger River.

1795   Lime juice was issued to all British sailors to prevent scurvy.

1796   English doctor Edward Jenner administered the first vaccination against smallpox to his gardener's son, James Phipps (aged eight). A single blister rose up on the spot, but James later demonstrated immunity to smallpox. Jenner actually used cowpox, a close viral relation to smallpox.

1797   The Spanish fleet was destroyed by the British under Admiral Jervis (with Nelson in support) at the battle of Cape St Vincent, off Portugal (Anglo-Spanish War, 1796–1808).

1798   The Marine Police Force was formed on the River Thames to prevent pilfering in the Port of London and West India Docks. It was one of the first organised police forces in Britain.

1799   Humphry Davy discovered the aesthetic properties of nitrous oxide. Known as laughing gas, it was often used for fun at parties of wealthy people. The scientist Davy believed this gas could be used to dull physical pain during minor surgery. The medical profession ignored this idea for nearly 50 years, until nitrous oxide eventually became the first medical anaesthetic.

1800   King George III survived a second assassination attempt.
        Doctor Benjamin Waterhouse (professor of Harvard Medical School) gave the cowpox vaccination to his son to prevent smallpox. He was the first doctor to test the smallpox vaccine in the United States.

1832   It wasn't until the Anatomy Act of 1832 that the taking of dead bodies from graves in Britain became officially illegal. Before then, removing corpses from a graveyard wasn't considered to be a crime, as a body had no legal status and wasn't actually owned by anyone. It was the robbing of valuables from graves that was illegal and why watchmen were employed at some graveyards. Physicians and medical students weren't particularly interested where the corpses they paid for came from, and the body-snatchers (also known as resurrectionists) kept their sources secret.

A sample from the thousands of recorded trials held in London from 1785–1805...

1795   CHRISTOPHER COLLINGS was accused
          of stealing, on the 31st August 1795,
          two pairs of silver shoe buckles, value 30
          shillings, the goods of Robert Chandler.

Witness statement: Between seven and eight o'clock in the evening, the prisoner at the bar came into the shop (we had lit all the lamps) and asked for a pair of buckles; I was so busy at that time with a lady I could not serve him. I left him stop about three minutes, just before I went to him. He said, 'Are you going to serve me?' On my going up to serve him I found the silver buckle drawer pulled open about twelve or fourteen inches; I told him that I suspected him taking a pair of silver buckles out of this drawer, and I insisted on searching his pockets. I found two pair of silver buckles in them.

Prisoner comment: I would be very glad to go to sea, to serve my King and country.
Verdict: GUILTY – aged twelve.
Sentence: Transported for seven years.

1799   HENRY MARR was accused of stealing, on the 3rd May 1799, a leather pocket-book, the property of George Warmington of Hook Norton in Oxfordshire, privily from his person.

Prisoner's defence: I was in Dufour's-place, there was a crowd collected, and they called out, stop thief, and, in the mob, I was pushed down, and close by my side there was a pocket-book found, and I was taken to the watch-house.
Verdict: GUILTY of stealing to the value of 10 pennies.
Sentence: Transported for seven years.

1800   JOHN STAUNTON was accused of stealing, on the 29th March 1800, a handkerchief, value 2 shillings, the property of John Maberly, privily from his person.

Prisoner's defence: I know nothing of it, I never had the handkerchief.
Verdict: GUILTY – aged 19.
Sentence: Transported for seven years.

1801:   SARAH LESTER was accused of stealing, on the 4th April 1801, a silk cloak and two yards of cotton, value 6 shillings, the property of James Tims, in his dwelling-house.

Prisoner's defence: I did not steal these things; I picked them up.
Verdict: GUILTY.
Sentence: Death – aged 22.

1801:   THOMAS BURRELL and JOHN WESKETT were accused of stealing, on 14th April 1801, 6 yards of printed cotton, value 12 shillings, the property of Robert Robinson and William Powell, in their shop.

Burrell's defence: There was a woman dropped the bundle at the corner of Turnstile, and I picked it up.
Verdict: Burrell, GUILTY.
Sentence: Death – aged 11.
Verdict: Weskett, GUILTY.
Sentence: Death – aged 10.

1801: JOSEPH ROBERTS, highwayman, was accused that he, in the King's highway, upon Thomas Milsum did make an assault on the 12th December 1801, putting him in fear, and taking from his person three shillings and twenty halfpence, the property of the said Thomas Milsum.

Verdict: GUILTY.
Sentence: Death - aged 26.

————

1803: MARY JONES was accused of stealing, on the 23rd April 1803, a pair of tongs, value 4 shillings, a pewter quart pot, value 14 pennies and a pewter pint pot, value 6 pennies, the property of Joseph Ivison.

Prisoner's defence: I am innocent of what I am accused of; a man came into the public house and put them into my pocket unknown to me.
Verdict: GUILTY – aged 40.
Sentence: Confined six months in the House of Correction and whipped.

1804   SARAH-ANN RAYFIELD was accused
of stealing, on the 21st July 1804, one
half-crown, one shilling, and twelve penny-
pieces, the property of Joseph Smith.

The prisoner called two witnesses, who gave her a
good character.

Verdict: GUILTY – aged 10.
Sentence: Whipped in jail and discharged

———————

1805:   JOHN HOFARD was accused of stealing,
on the 18th July 1805, eleven pounds
weight of rope, value 5 shillings, the
property of John Shepherd Killick of
Hackney Mills, Lea Bridge.

Verdict: GUILTY - aged 25.
Sentence: Transported for seven years.

GLOSSARY

Bow Street Runner
The first police in London. In response to the high level of crime in London in 1750, men known as Bow Street Runners were paid to patrol the streets within the parish of Bow Street.

Cadaver
A dead body.

Cherub
An angel, often shown as a child with two wings (cherubim = more than one cherub, cherubic = like a cherub).

Inoculate
To introduce material (such as a virus) into the body to protect against or treat a disease.

Laudanum
A mixture of alcohol and morphine that was once used as a painkiller.

Omnipotent
Having unlimited power.

Pillory
A wooden frame with holes in it in which the head and hands are locked, and once used for the public punishment of wrongdoers.

Ragamuffin
A poorly clothed and dirty child.

Resurrectionist
A body-snatcher who unearthed and stole dead bodies, especially for dissection or medical research.

Seraph
An angel, often shown with six wings (seraphim = more than one seraph).

Variola
(from Latin *varius* meaning spotted) A disease marked by spots and blisters; namely smallpox, cowpox and horsepox.

A selected list of Scribo titles

The prices shown below are correct at the time of going to press. However, The Salariya Book Company reserves the right to show new retail prices on covers, which may differ from those previously advertised.

The Long-Lost Secret Diary

of the World's Worst... by Tim Collins

Knight	978-1-912006-67-0	£6.99
Pirate	978-1-912006-66-3	£6.99
Astronaut	978-1-912233-20-5	£6.99
Dinosaur Hunter	978-1-912233-19-9	£6.99

Gladiator School by Dan Scott

1 Blood Oath	978-1-908177-48-3	£6.99
2 Blood & Fire	978-1-908973-60-3	£6.99
3 Blood & Sand	978-1-909645-16-5	£6.99
4 Blood Vengeance	978-1-909645-62-2	£6.99
5 Blood & Thunder	978-1-910184-20-2	£6.99
6 Blood Justice	978-1-910184-43-1	£6.99

Iron Sky by Alex Woolf

1 Dread Eagle	978-1-909645-00-4	£9.99
2 Call of the Phoenix	978-1-910184-87-5	£6.99